THE
OTHER MAN

Francis Durbridge

WILLIAMS & WHITING

Cover design by Timo Schroeder

9781912582549

Williams & Whiting (Publishers)
15 Chestnut Grove, Hurstpierpoint,
West Sussex, BN6 9SS

Titles by Francis Durbridge published by Williams & Whiting

1   The Scarf – tv serial
2   Paul Temple and the Curzon Case – radio serial
3   La Boutique – radio serial
4   The Broken Horseshoe – tv serial
5   Three Plays for Radio Volume 1
6   Send for Paul Temple – radio serial
7   A Time of Day – tv serial
8   Death Comes to The Hibiscus – stage play
    The Essential Heart – radio play
    (writing as Nicholas Vane)
9   Send for Paul Temple – stage play
10 The Teckman Biography (tv serial)
11 Paul Temple and Steve (radio serial)
12 Twenty Minutes From Rome
13 Portrait of Alison
14 Paul Temple: Two Plays for Radio Volume 1
15 Three Plays for Radio Volume 2

Murder At The Weekend – the rediscovered newspaper serials and short stories

Also published by Williams & Whiting:
Francis Durbridge : The Complete Guide
By Melvyn Barnes

A Case For Paul Temple
A Game of Murder
A Man Called Harry Brent
Bat Out of Hell
Breakaway – The Family Affair
Breakaway – The Local Affair
Melissa

Murder In The Media
One Man To Another – a novel
My Friend Charles
Paul Temple and the Alex Affair
Paul Temple and the Canterbury Case (film script)
Paul Temple and the Conrad Case
Paul Temple and the Geneva Mystery
Paul Temple and the Gilbert Case
Paul Temple and the Gregory Affair
Paul Temple and the Jonathan Mystery
Paul Temple and the Lawrence Affair
Paul Temple and the Madison Mystery
Paul Temple and the Margo Mystery
Paul Temple and the Spencer Affair
Paul Temple and the Sullivan Mystery
Paul Temple and the Vandyke Affair
Paul Temple Intervenes
Step In The Dark
The Desperate People
The Doll
One Man To Another – a novel
The World of Tim Frazer
Tim Frazer and the Salinger Affair
Tim Frazer and the Mellin Forrest Mystery
Two Paul Temple Plays for Television

INTRODUCTION

The career of playwright Francis Durbridge (1912-98) was impressive in both duration and versatility, and many might be unaware of its extent. While remembering his television serials from the 1950s onwards, some might not know that at that stage he was already the most popular writer of mystery thrillers for BBC radio from as early as the 1930s.

In 1938 he firmly established his name with the radio serial *Send for Paul Temple*, which was so successful that it led to a series that continued for thirty years and created an enormous UK and European fanbase. Paul Temple and his wife Steve became icons of popular culture, and as well as pursuing master criminals on twenty-eight occasions on the radio they appeared in a daily newspaper strip in the London *Evening News* from 11 December 1950 to 1 May 1971 that was syndicated throughout the UK and abroad.

Francis Durbridge, while continuing to write for radio, turned to the small screen in 1952 with *The Broken Horseshoe* and record books define this as the first thriller serial on British television. And to complete this summary of his career, from 1946 to 1957 his radio and television serials led to nine British cinema films and from the 1970s he became known to theatregoers for skillfully plotted stage plays.

The Other Man, Durbridge's sixth BBC television serial and one of his best, was shown in six thirty-minute episodes from 20 October to 24 November 1956. It was repeated from 20 February to 27 March 1957, so there must have been a recording that afterwards died at the hands of the BBC wipers as no DVDs have ever been marketed. The producer/director, Alan Bromly, was to remain the guru for most of Durbridge's television serials, just as Martyn C. Webster had done for his radio serials. The Durbridge/Bromly partnership, dating from the fourth television serial *Portrait of Alison* in 1955, could always be relied upon to provide traditional Durbridge ingredients - numerous red herrings, a stunning cliff-hanger at the end of each episode, and the certainty that viewers should not believe anything that anyone says.

As always with Durbridge's television serials, *The Other Man* boasted a quality cast – headed by Tony Britton (1924-2019) in his first Durbridge role, although he was to return in *Melissa* in 1964. Clearly Britton became a Durbridge fan, as he said (*Radio Times*, 23 April 1964): "He constructs a plot like a solidly built house … with twisting passages leading to strange rooms. He never telegraphs where the story may lead to next, and just when it seems to be taking a straightforward course you're slapped in the face with a fabulous cliffhanger." And the actor Duncan Lamont (1918-78), appearing as Inspector Ford, gives rise to two interesting points – firstly he was married to Patricia Driscoll (1927-2020), who played Katherine Walters in *The Other Man*; and secondly he had previously played Inspector Hilton in the Durbridge film *The Teckman Mystery* (1954).

Francis Durbridge was the foremost exponent of the thriller serial on UK television, the master of plots that twisted and turned while his protagonist struggled in a web spun by someone who remained a mystery until the final episode. But another aspect of Durbridge thrillers was their "Britishness" at a time when many television crime series were imported from the USA – a factor that also applied to Durbridge's nearest television rival, Nigel Kneale, whose serials featuring Professor Bernard Quatermass were also massively popular. Indeed, in his obituary of Kneale (*The Independent*, 2 November 2006), Jack Adrian stated that: "During the 1950s and 1960s Nigel Kneale bestrode the world of British television like a colossus (and) the only writer who came anywhere near him in terms of sheer entertainment and popularity was Francis Durbridge."

For many years since the 1930s, Durbridge radio serials were broadcast in various European countries in their own languages and using their own actors. It was therefore not surprising that he also became a great attraction on European television screens, beginning when *The Other Man* was adapted for German television in 1959 as *Der Andere* (5 – 16 October 1959, six episodes), translated by Marianne de Barde and directed by Joachim Hoene. And much later *The Other Man* appeared on Italian television as *Lungo il fiume e sull'acqua* (13 – 27 January 1973, five episodes), translated by Franca Cancogni, adapted by Biagio Proietti and directed by Alberto Negrin.

Every Durbridge television serial following *The Other Man* was seen throughout Europe – usually translated but sometimes dubbing the UK original – and they attracted enormous audiences. In fact he achieved iconic status when German commentators described his serials as *straßenfeger* (street sweepers), because a great swathe of the population stayed at home to listen to them on the radio or watch them on television.

As mentioned above, adaptations of Durbridge serials for the cinema proved popular – and viewers of Talking Pictures TV still have the opportunity to see them today. From 1946 onwards, four film adaptations of his early Paul Temple radio serials were made and were followed by film versions of his first five BBC television serials *The Broken Horseshoe, Operation Diplomat, The Teckman Biography* (filmed as *The Teckman Mystery*), *Portrait of Alison* and *My Friend Charles* (filmed as *The Vicious Circle*). But sadly the cinema world appears to have lost interest in Durbridge after the mid-1950s (not sensational enough?), whereas his radio and television careers and later his theatrical career proceeded apace.

The Other Man was published as a novel (Hodder & Stoughton, October 1958) and European translations have appeared in Germany as *Der Andere*, in Holland as *De andere man*, in France as *L'Autre Homme*, in Italy *as Lungo il fiume e sull'acqua*, in Spain as *El otro hombre*, in Sweden as *I de lugnaste vattnen* and in Poland as *Ten drugi*.

But in the absence of a television recording, let's enjoy this discovery of his original television script!

Melvyn Barnes
Author of *Francis Durbridge: The Complete Guide* (Williams & Whiting, 2018)

This book reproduces Francis Durbridge's original script together with the list of characters and actors of the BBC programme on the dates mentioned, but the eventual broadcast might have edited Durbridge's script in respect of scenes, dialogue and character names.

THE OTHER MAN

A serial in SIX episodes

By FRANCIS DURBRIDGE

Broadcast on BBC Television

20 October – 24 November 1956

CAST:

David Henderson . . . . Tony Britton

Roger Ford . . . . David Tilley

Mrs. Williams . . . . Brenda Cowling

James Cooper . . . . John Kidd

Katherine Walters . . . . . Patricia Driscoll

Det.-Insp. Ford . . . . Duncan Lamont

Det.-Sgt. Broderick . . . . . . Victor Brooks

Judy . . . . Brenda Dean

Dr. Sheldon . . . . Jack Lambert

Ralph Merson . . . . Peter Copley

Billie Reynolds . . . . Vanda Godsell

Robin Craven . . . . Philip Guard

Chris Reynolds . . . . Ian Whittaker

P.C. Sanders . . . . Ronald Baddiley

Maria Rocello . . . . Marla Landi

Harry Vincent . . . . John Arnatt

EPISODE ONE

OPEN TO: The grounds and quadrangle of Buckingham College, a large English Public School on the outskirts of Medlow, Bucks, England.

Superimpose the following quotation:
"He that has a secret should not only hide it, but hide that he has it to hide"   Carlyle

Fade quotation as DAVID HENDERSON appears on the path leading up towards the main building of the school. HENDERSON is a good-looking man in his late thirties; he wears a dark suit, a gown, and carries a Latin dictionary and about half a dozen exercise books. A boy stops HENDERSON and speaks to him; HENDERSON nods, gives the boy one of the exercise books and then continues up the path towards the school. HENDERSON enters the school.

CUT TO: HENDERSON's Private Study at the College.
It is a large, well-furnished, bachelor-looking room. There is an abundance of books, magazines, newspapers, etc.
ROGER FORD, an intelligent looking boy of about fifteen, is standing near the desk reading a book. He looks up as HENDERSON enters. HENDERSON looks at ROGER, takes off his gown and hangs it on a peg on the door.
HENDERSON: Hello, Ford! Have you been waiting long?
ROGER: No, sir.
HENDERSON crosses to the desk; he is watching ROGER.
HENDERSON: Well – I've spoken to Mr Granger.
ROGER: (*Anxiously*) Yes, sir?
HENDERSON: Since we break up on Tuesday, he's prepared to overlook the matter.
ROGER: (*Relieved*) Oh, thank you, sir.
HENDERSON: Don't thank me – thank Mr Granger. But next time you see Justin 11 bending over the

	swimming pool, control your natural impulses, Ford.
ROGER:	(*Smiling*) I'll try to, sir.
HENDERSON:	Justin weighs fourteen stone; he was never meant to be a flying saucer.
ROGER:	I realise that now, sir.

HENDERSON puts the exercise books down on the desk, opens one and glances down at it.

HENDERSON:	Is anyone picking you up on Tuesday morning?
ROGER:	Yes, sir. My father. (*Hesitantly*) I said I'd be ready by seven o'clock. Is that all right, sir?
HENDERSON:	It's all right by me, Ford – but I can't speak for your father.
ROGER:	Oh, he'll be here, sir.
HENDERSON:	Seven o'clock sounds excessively early, even for a detective inspector.
ROGER:	My father's a very early riser, sir.

HENDERSON gives ROGER a look. MRS WILLIAMS, HENDERSON's housekeeper, enters. She is a pleasant looking woman in her late fifties.

HENDERSON:	Yes, Mrs Williams – what is it?
MRS WILLIAMS:	(*Offering HENDERSON a small brown paper package*) There's a registered package for you, sir.
HENDERSON:	(*Taking the package*) Oh, thank you.
MRS WILLIAMS:	I'm just slipping down into Medlow, Mr Henderson. I won't be very long.
HENDERSON:	Yes, all right, Mrs Williams.

MRS WILLIAMS goes out. HENDERSON looks at the package, then glances up at ROGER.

HENDERSON:	(*Dismissing ROGER*) All right, Ford. You can go. If you see Mr Granger, tell him I've spoken to you.

4

ROGER: Yes, sir. (*He hesitates*)

HENDERSON starts to unwrap the parcel then realises that ROGER is hesitating; he looks up.

HENDERSON: Well?

ROGER: (*Opening the book he is carrying*) Excuse me, sir. What does this mean?

HENDERSON: What?

ROGER: (*Reading from the book*) Suavitor in modo …

HENDERSON: (*A shade surprised by the question*) Suavitor in modo?

ROGER: Yes, sir.

HENDERSON: Well – it means – Gentle in the manner …

ROGER: (*Looking at the book again; puzzled*) Suavitor in modo, fortiter in re …

HENDERSON: (*Nodding*) That's right. Suavitor in modo, fortiter in re … Gentle in the manner, but vigorous in the deed.

HENDERSON puts the package down on the desk and crosses to ROGER.

HENDERSON: (*Quietly*) Is that in the book I lent you?

ROGER: (*Showing HENDERSON the book*) Yes, sir. You've written it on the flyleaf. I wondered what it meant, sir.

HENDERSON: (*After a moment; quietly*) Well, now you know, Ford. (*His thoughts elsewhere*) Gentle in the manner, but vigorous in the deed …

ROGER: (*A shade puzzled by HENDERSON's manner*) Yes, sir.

HENDERSON: (*Suddenly; nodding*) All right. You can go.

ROGER: Thank you, sir.

ROGER goes out, watched by HENDERSON. After a moment, HENDERSON returns to the desk and picks up the package; he unwraps the package and takes out a man's wristlet watch. He stands looking at the watch, then he puts it down on the desk,

5

takes a bunch of keys from his pocket, and crosses to the door. He locks the door with one of the keys and returns to the desk.

HENDERSON looks at the watch again, then he takes off his own wristlet watch on his wrist. He then unlocks a drawer in the desk and takes out a small leather notebook and an automatic pistol. His manner is perfectly natural; unhurried, not in any way tense or dramatic. He puts his own watch in the drawer and places the book and the revolver on the desk.

The telephone rings. HENDERSON hesitates, then lifts the receiver.

HENDERSON:	(*On the phone*) Hello? … Henderson speaking …
COOPER:	(*On the other end of the phone; a polite, educated voice*) This is Cooper …
HENDERSON:	(*Quietly, pleasantly*) Oh, hello … I was just going to phone you.
COOPER:	Have you got the watch?
HENDERSON:	Yes, it's just arrived. Are we in time?
COOPER:	(*Hesitates*) I – think so. Anyway, we'll have to take a chance on it. Will three o'clock suit you?
HENDERSON:	Yes, I'll be there.
COOPER:	(*Politely*) Thank you, Henderson.

We hear the receiver being replaced. HENDERSON replaces the telephone and looks at the wristlet watch he is wearing.

CUT TO: A Houseboat on a pleasant stretch of the river near Medlow. The boat is called High Tor.

DAVID HENDERSON appears from the living quarters below and stands on the deck looking towards the open country. (He is looking for a car which is parked in a nearby country lane)

Suddenly he sees what he is looking for and gives a significant wave of the hand. He turns and goes below deck.

CUT TO: The main cabin of the houseboat. The cabin is well furnished but at the moment it is extremely untidy, almost a shambles; it gives the impression of having recently been ransacked.

HENDERSON enters and stands in the doorway for a moment, then he crosses the cabin to where the body of a man can be seen on the floor. The man is fully dressed, his face turned away from HENDERSON. We do not see his face.

HENDERSON kneels by the body and slowly takes off the wristlet watch he is wearing, and straps it onto the wrist of the dead man. He rises, looks round the cabin, then turns and crosses towards the door.

CUT TO: *KATHERINE WALTERS, an attractive girl in her late twenties, is sitting in a punt reading a novel. The punt is under a tree about fifty yards down river from the houseboat. KATHERINE looks up from her novel and looks at the houseboat.*

We see HENDERSON come on deck and a car draw level with the houseboat. From KATHERINE's position in the punt it is impossible to see the driver of the car but HENDERSON can be seen quite clearly as he leaves the house and climbs into the car. The car drives away from the houseboat and the river.

CUT TO: *The dead man in the cabin of the houseboat. The camera tracks back to reveal MORRIS, a plain clothes detective, taking measurements of the cabin and the exact position of the body. DETECTIVE INSPECTOR FORD is at the opposite end of the cabin examining the contents of a small writing bureau. FORD is a pleasant, serious-looking man in his early forties. MORRIS rises from the floor.*

7

MORRIS: (*To FORD*) Is there anything else, sir?

FORD: No. Tell Jackson he can go ahead now.

MORRIS: Right, sir.

DETECTIVE SERGEANT BRODERICK enters.

BRODERICK: (*To MORRIS*) Jackson wants to know how long you're going to be?

MORRIS: I've just finished.

MORRIS goes out.

BRODERICK: (*To FORD*) Has the doctor been, sir?

FORD: (*Turning from the desk; a shade irritated*) Yes, he's been. They sent Jennings.

BRODERICK: Oh Lord! Well – what did he say?

FORD: The usual story. Impossible to say without an autopsy, even then it might be difficult.

BRODERICK: (*With sarcasm*) I suppose he is dead.

FORD: (*Smiling*) Oh, he's dead all right. Even Jennings had to admit that.

BRODERICK: I'm surprised he went that far.

FORD: Well – what happened? Did you make inquiries?

BRODERICK: (*Taking out a notebook*) His name's Rocello; he's an Italian. He's been down here nearly a fortnight. The houseboat belongs to a man called Cooper … James Cooper.

FORD: I know Cooper. I've seen him in the village. Tall, distinguished looking chap, rather a long nose.

BRODERICK: Yes, that's the fellow. Apparently he's a solicitor; works for a firm called (*Looks at his notebook*) … Dawson, Wyman and Clewes.

FORD: Are they in London?

BRODERICK: Yes – Sloane Square.

FORD: Was Rocello a friend of Cooper's?

BRODERICK: It looks like it. According to Mrs Prothero – she keeps the tobacconists in the High Street – Cooper went back to Town last Wednesday and

	left Rocello down here in charge of the houseboat.
FORD:	(*Thoughtfully*) Last Wednesday? Didn't Cooper come down for the weekend?
BRODERICK:	Not according to Mrs Prothero.
FORD:	Would she know?
BRODERICK:	Yes, I think so. She has two or three lock-ups and Cooper usually parks his car in one of them.
FORD:	I see.

BRODERICK looks down at the body.

| BRODERICK: | Well, whoever did it, certainly made a nice job of it … |

JACKSON, the police photographer, enters. He carries photographic equipment.

| FORD: | (*Thoughtfully*) Yes. (*Dismissing BRODERICK*) All right, Sergeant. You know the drill. (*To JACKSON*) Go ahead, Jackson. |

JACKSON takes up a position near the body and raises the camera. There is a 'flash' as he photographs the body.

CUT TO: A Small Brass Plate attached to the gate of a country house. The plate reads: Dr Terence Sheldon, M.D. The camera tracks back to reveal a short drive leading up to the house.
A police car arrives and stops at the entrance to the drive. DETECTIVE INSPECTOR FORD gets out of the car and walks up the drive.

CUT TO: The Living Room of DR SHELDON's House.
FORD is shown into the room by JUDY, a young parlourmaid.

JUDY:	Dr Sheldon won't keep you long, sir.
FORD:	Thank you.
JUDY:	Shall I take your hat and coat?
FORD:	No, thank you, Judy.

JUDY goes out. FORD takes stock of his surroundings; crosses to the French windows. He stands looking out into the garden, then turns as DR SHELDON enters. SHELDON is a pleasant man in his early fifties.

SHELDON: Good morning!

FORD: (*Turning*) Oh, good morning, sir! It's very kind of you to see me at such short notice.

SHELDON: What can I do for you, Inspector?

FORD: I understand you have a young lady staying with you, sir – a Miss Walters.

SHELDON: Yes, that's right. She's my niece.

FORD: Do you think I could have a word with her, sir?

SHELDON: (*Puzzled*) Yes, by all means. (*Crosses and opens the door; calling*) Judy, tell Miss Katherine to come into the drawing room.

FORD: I'm investigating a murder case, Doctor. You've probably read about it. A man was found murdered on one of the houseboats.

SHELDON: Yes, I was talking to Katherine – Miss Walters – about it only this morning. He was an Italian, wasn't he?

FORD: That's right. He name was Rocello – Paul Rocello. He was staying with a Mr Cooper.

SHELDON: I think I met Cooper about six months ago. Tall, distinguished chap. He's a solicitor.

FORD: That's right, sir.

SHELDON: Was this Italian, the murdered man, a friend of his?

FORD: We believe so, although unfortunately we haven't been able to contact Cooper, so our information's rather second-hand at the moment.

SHELDON: I thought Cooper worked for a firm called Dawson, Wyman and Clewes?

10

FORD: Yes, that's what we thought, sir. (*Pleasantly, changing the subject*) I'll tell you why I wanted a word with Miss Walters, Doctor. I understand she hired a punt on Thursday and spent an hour or so on the river.

SHELDON: Did she? I know she went out on Thursday afternoon. I didn't know she went on the river.

FORD: I think she did, sir. (*Takes his notebook out of his pocket*) She hired the punt from Barker Brothers. She went out about half past two and returned at about four o'clock. At least that's according to our information.

SHELDON: (*Smiling*) I'm sure your information's correct, Inspector.

FORD: (*Closing the notebook*) I don't think I've met Miss Walters before, have I, Doctor?

SHELDON: No, she's only been staying with me three or four days. Her father, my brother, died rather suddenly about two weeks ago and unfortunately –

FORD: Oh, I'm sorry to hear that, sir.

SHELDON: Yes, the whole thing was a dreadful shock to us. Katherine was abroad at the time and I had an awful job finding …

SHELDON breaks off at KATHERINE enters. He turns towards her.

SHELDON: Oh, here you are, my dear. Katherine, this is Inspector Ford.

FORD: (*Shaking hands with KATHERINE*) How do you do, Miss Walters?

KATHERINE: (*Pleasantly*) Good morning, Inspector.

SHELDON: Katherine, Inspector Ford is investigating that murder case – the one we were talking about at

11

breakfast this morning. He wants to ask you a few questions.

KATHERINE: (*Puzzled*) Ask – me?

FORD: Yes. (*Smiling*) It's just a routine enquiry, Miss Walters. I understand you spent part of Thursday afternoon on the river?

KATHERINE: Yes, I did. It was a lovely afternoon, so I hired a punt.

FORD: (*Nodding, smiling*) One of the tradespeople saw you. He said you were marooned or parked or whatever the word is, about fifty yards from High Tor.

KATHERINE: High Tor?

FORD: Yes, that's the houseboat. The one where the murder was committed.

KATHERINE: (*Surprised*) Good gracious! Was that the houseboat? A grey looking monstrosity with a green flag?

FORD: That's right, Miss Walters.

KATHERINE: I never knew that was the boat. Why, the newspaper I read said it was almost opposite the weir.

FORD: (*Shaking his head*) No, it's about half a mile from Barker Brothers. There are one or two houseboats on that stretch of the river.

KATHERINE: Yes, of course. I remember now.

FORD: Well, the point is, Miss Walters, did you see anything or hear anything on Thursday which aroused your suspicions in any way?

KATHERINE: No. It was a particularly pleasant afternoon. I read most of the time.

SHELDON: What time was the murder committed, Inspector?

FORD:	It's difficult to say, sir. Probably between one o'clock on Wednesday morning and four o'clock on Thursday afternoon.
SHELDON:	That's not very definite, Inspector.
FORD:	It's the best Dr Jennings could do for us, sir.
SHELDON:	I see. How was he murdered? Was he shot?
FORD:	No, there was a struggle, and he was hit across the face with something, probably with the butt end of a revolver. Whoever did it made quite a job of it. (*Dismissing the matter*) Well, I take it you can't help us, Miss Walters?
KATHERINE:	(*Hesitantly*) No, I'm afraid I can't.
FORD:	You didn't see, or hear, anything?
KATHERINE:	Nothing suspicious. I saw the car, of course.
FORD:	Which car?
KATHERINE:	A car drove up to the houseboat at about half-past three and a man got into it.
FORD:	Did you see this man?
KATHERINE:	Yes, of course.
FORD:	Did you recognise him?
KATHERINE:	No, I'd never seen him before.
FORD:	Who was driving the car?
KATHERINE:	I don't know. I didn't really take a lot of notice. I saw the car drive up and I saw the man get into it, but I couldn't tell you who was driving.
FORD:	What sort of a car was it?
KATHERINE:	Oh dear, I really don't know.
FORD:	Was it a saloon?
KATHERINE:	Yes.
FORD:	What colour?
KATHERINE:	It was black, I think, or dark blue.
FORD:	You say this happened at about half-past three?
KATHERINE:	Yes. Certainly no later.
FORD:	Describe this man, Miss Walters.

13

KATHERINE:	(*Thoughtfully*) Well, I should say he was fairly tall; slim, about forty. He wore a light overcoat.
FORD:	Would you recognise him again, if you saw him?
KATHERINE:	(*After a moment, thoughtfully*) Yes, I think I would, Inspector.

CUT TO: DAVID HENDERSON's study. Night.

HENDERSON is sitting at his desk correcting several exercise books. There is a small tray on the desk containing a pot of coffee and a copy of the evening newspaper. MRS WILLIAMS enters.

MRS WILLIAMS:	Excuse me. Mr Ford would like to see you, sir.
HENDERSON:	(*Looking up*) Mr Ford?
MRS WILLIAMS:	Yes, he said he'd like to have a word with you, sir, if you could spare him a few minutes.
HENDERSON:	Yes, certainly. Ask him in, Mrs Williams.

MRS WILLIAMS goes out and a moment later shows in INSPECTOR FORD. HENDERSON rises and crosses to FORD. MRS WILLIAMS goes out again.

HENDERSON:	(*Shaking hands with FORD*) Hello, Inspector. This is a pleasant surprise.
FORD:	I hope I haven't disturbed you.
HENDERSON:	No, not at all. I was just having some coffee. Would you like some?
FORD:	No, thank you, sir.
HENDERSON:	Oh, before I forget – Roger's expecting you on Tuesday morning. Seven o'clock.
FORD:	(*Smiling*) Yes, I know. I've had a letter from the young rascal. How's he getting on?

14

HENDERSON indicates a chair and FORD sits down.

HENDERSON: Oh, splendidly! His Latin's still a little shaky, I'm afraid, but it'll be all right.

FORD: He said you'd been giving him extra coaching, sir.

HENDERSON: Oh, just an odd half hour every now and again. It all helps. Was it Roger you wanted to see me about?

FORD: No, it was something quite different. I expect that you've read about this murder case? The Italian chap.

HENDERSON: Yes, I have. Extraordinary business.

FORD: Well, I'm investigating the case and I suddenly remember your telling me that you'd spent a certain amount of time in Italy – Venice, I believe you said, sir.

HENDERSON: Yes, I was there for two years. April '44 to December '46.

FORD: Well, we think this chap Rocello – Paul Rochello – came from Venice, and I was wondering if you'd heard the name?

HENDERSON: (*Amused*) Venice isn't a village, Inspector.

FORD: (*Smiling*) I know, sir. I'm not suggesting that you might have heard of Rocello himself, it's the name I'm curious about. I wondered whether it was a fairly common one in those parts.

HENDERSON: Rocello? Sounds as if it might be. (*Shaking his head*) I don't think I've heard it before.

FORD: (*Pleasantly*) I see. Thank you, Mr Henderson.

HENDERSON: (*Faintly surprised*) Is that all, Inspector?

FORD:	No. (*Smiling*) This is what I really wanted to see you about. (*He takes a piece of paper from his pocket*)
HENDERSON:	What is it?
FORD:	It's an inscription. It was written on the back of the dead man's wristlet watch. The Superintendent had a shot of it, but his Latin's even worse than mine, I'm afraid.

HENDERSON takes the sheet of paper and looks at it.

HENDERSON:	(*After a moment, quietly reading*) Suavitor in modo, fortiter in re. (*Looking up quite pleasantly*) It means: Gentle in the manner, but vigorous in the deed.
FORD:	Gentle in the manner, but vigorous in the deed?
HENDERSON:	(*Smiling*) That's right, Inspector.
FORD:	Well, the gentleman who committed the murder was certainly vigorous in the deed. He smashed the poor devil's face in. (*He takes the piece of paper*) Well, thank you, Mr Henderson. Sorry to have troubled you.
HENDERSON:	No trouble, Inspector. I should think this is a pretty interesting case, isn't it?
FORD:	(*Rising*) It's a very puzzling one, sir. You see, Cooper – he's the man who owns the houseboat – seems to be something of an enigma. Everyone down here thought he was a solicitor, and worked for a firm called Dawson, Wyman and Clewes.
HENDERSON:	Well, doesn't he?
FORD:	No, they've never even heard of him.
HENDERSON:	Oh.

FORD:	(*Confidentially*) Don't repeat that, sir – that's just between ourselves.
HENDERSON:	Yes, of course. Well, I wish you joy, Inspector. I'm glad you're investigating the case, and not me.
FORD:	(*As he moves towards the door*) Yes. Still we musn't grumble. We've had one slice of luck.
HENDERSON:	Oh, really?
FORD:	Yes, a girl called Katherine Walters – she's a niece of Dr Sheldon's – happened to be on the river on Thursday afternoon and she saw a car drive up to the houseboat.
HENDERSON:	Oh, what time was that?
FORD:	About half past three.
HENDERSON:	Did anyone get out of the car?
FORD:	No, but apparently someone got into it. (*Suddenly, looks at the piece of paper he is holding*) Look, what did you say this was? Gentle in the manner …?
HENDERSON:	(*Quietly; unperturbed, pleasantly*) Gentle in the manner, but vigorous in the deed. (*He takes the paper from FORD*) I'll write it down for you.

HENDERSON crosses to his desk and scribbles the words on the piece of paper.

HENDERSON:	(*Handing FORD the piece of paper*) Here we are, Inspector.
FORD:	Thank you, sir. It's very kind of you. Good night, Mr Henderson.
HENDERSON:	(*Smiling*) Good night. I'll tell Roger I've seen you.

17

FORD smiles and goes out. HENDERSON returns to his desk, picks up his pen and opens one of the exercise books. He makes a correction in the book, then looks up; after a moment's reflection he pours himself a cup of coffee. He holds the cup in both hands, staring down at it. He appears thoughtful but not in any way perturbed.

CUT TO: The Main Entrance of Buckingham College.
DR SHELDON complete with black homburg, bag, etc., comes out of the building and crosses to his car which is parked in front of the College. KATHERINE is sitting in the car waiting for her uncle. SHELDON smiles at KATHERINE and gets into the driving seat of the car.

CUT TO: The Tennis Courts of Buckingham College.
DAVID HENDERSON and a colleague have just finished playing a game of tennis and are leaving the courts. As they walk back towards the main school building DR SHELDON drives past in his car. He gives a friendly wave to HENDERSON who returns the greeting. Suddenly KATHERINE turns her head and looks back at the two men. HENDERSON does not notice her, he is in conversation with his friend.

CUT TO: *A police car brakes to a standstill outside of DR SHELDON's house. FORD gets out of the car and walks briskly up the drive.*

CUT TO: The Living Room of DR SHELDON's House.
SHELDON is stood near the open French windows looking out into the garden; he looks puzzled and worried. KATHERINE is sitting on the settee.
KATHERINE: Was that a car?

SHELDON: Yes, I think this is the Inspector. (*He turns and looks at KATHERINE*) Katherine, you're sure now, aren't you?

KATHERINE: (*With just a faint suggestion of irritation*) Uncle, I've told you at least half a dozen times, I'm absolutely sure!

SHELDON: (*Worried*) Of course, there may be a perfectly simple explanation.

KATHERINE: (*Rising and crossing to SHELDON*) I'm sure there is a perfectly simple explanation. On the other hand, I've got to tell the Inspector, haven't I?

SHELDON: Yes, of course, my dear. It's only that Henderson's a patient of mine, and naturally … (*Breaking off; calling through the French windows*) Inspector!

FORD enters through the French windows.

FORD: (*Pleasantly*)   Good   afternoon,   Doctor. (*Smiling at KATHERINE*) Hello, Miss Walters.

There is a slight pause. SHELDON looks at KATHERINE. He is a shade uncomfortable.

FORD: I received a telephone message saying you wanted to see me, sir. It sounded urgent.

SHELDON: (*Hesitantly*) Yes … I … er … Do sit down, Inspector.

FORD looks at SHELDON with interest, then across at KATHERINE. He sits down.

FORD: What is it you want to see me about, sir?

SHELDON: I had to go up to the school this morning to see the Bursar. He's suffering from hay fever, and I've been giving him injections. Well, to cut a long story short, Katherine was with me.

19

	On the way home we passed two of the staff – they'd been playing tennis.
FORD:	(*Interested*) Go on, sir.
SHELDON:	Katherine recognised one of them. She said it was the man she saw on Thursday. The man on the houseboat.
FORD:	(*Quietly, yet obviously surprised*) Are you sure, Miss Walters?
KATHERINE:	Yes, I'm quite sure.
FORD:	(*To SHELDON*) Well, who was it? You know most of the Buckingham people.
SHELDON:	It was Mr Henderson.
FORD:	(*Astonished*) Henderson!
SHELDON:	(*Quietly*) Yes.
FORD:	(*A little laugh*) Oh, but that's impossible! It couldn't have been Henderson.
SHELDON:	I'm afraid it was, Inspector.

FORD looks at SHELDON, then across at KATHERINE.

FORD:	(*To KATHERINE, quietly*) Are you sure, Miss Walters?
KATHERINE:	I'm quite sure.
SHELDON:	When Katherine told me I didn't know what on earth to do. I thought at first I ought to have a word with Henderson. You see, he's a patient of mine, and I didn't want him to think …
FORD:	(*Interrupting*) Did you have a word with him?
SHELDON:	No. Katherine advised me not to.

FORD looks across at KATHERINE.

FORD:	(*After a moment*) Miss Walters, have you a very good memory for faces?
KATHERINE:	Yes, I have.
FORD:	Supposing you were confronted by Mr Henderson and five or six other men – men of

	a similar height and build and appearance – do you think you'd be able to identify him?
KATHERINE:	Yes, I do.

FORD hesitates, looks across at SHELDON and then back at KATHERINE.

KATHERINE:	(*Faintly irritated*) You think I've made a mistake, don't you?
FORD:	No. No, I wouldn't go so far as to say that, Miss Walters. But I do think …
KATHERINE:	(*Interrupting him*) Inspector, tell me: is this Mr Henderson a friend of yours?

FORD is surprised by the question; he looks at KATHERINE for a moment before replying.

FORD:	Yes, I suppose you'd call him a friend. Why?
KATHERINE:	I wondered, that's all.

SHELDON glances at the INSPECTOR: he is a shade embarrassed.

FORD:	(*Looking at KATHERINE; quietly*) Two years ago, when my wife died, I was in a quandary. My boy was thirteen, he was at day school, and I just didn't know what on earth to do with him. One day I bumped into Henderson and he suggested Buckingham. I knew Rog was a clever kid but, for various reasons, I didn't think he had a chance, not for a Buckingham scholarship. Henderson thought otherwise.
SHELDON:	(*Nodding*) He's an awfully nice chap, Katherine.
KATHERINE:	I'm sure he's an awfully nice chap, and I'm sure he didn't commit the murder – but he was at the houseboat. I saw him!
FORD:	You haven't spoken to anyone else about this, have you?

21

KATHERINE: No, of course not.

FORD looks at SHELDON who shakes his head.

SHELDON: (*With a little laugh*) You know, I'm sure there's a simple explanation. Perhaps Henderson's a friend of Cooper's. He called to see him and found that he was out.

KATHERINE: Then he must have seen the body …

SHELDON: Oh no, not necessarily, Katherine.

FORD: (*Quietly*) I saw Henderson yesterday afternoon. We talked about the murder, the houseboat. He never said he was a friend of Cooper's.

SHELDON: Did you ask him?

FORD: No, not exactly, but surely he'd have mentioned it. (*Suddenly, holding out his hand to KATHERINE*) Well – thank you, Miss Walters. It's very good of you to help us like this. (*Smiling*) Don't think we don't appreciate it. I take it you'll be staying down here for some little time?

KATHERINE: Well, certainly for the next week or two.

FORD: We'll be in touch with you. (*Nods to SHELDON*) Good afternoon, Doctor.

FORD goes out through the French windows. KATHERINE stands looking after him.

CUT TO: DAVID HENDERSON's Study.

HENDERSON is sitting in the armchair, smoking a pipe and reading a book. He looks quite happy and contented. There is a knock on the door which he doesn't hear. After a moment the knock is repeated and he looks up.

HENDERSON: (*Calling*) Come in .

The door opens and FORD enters. He looks serious and a shade perturbed. HENDERSON is pleasantly surprised and rises from the chair.

HENDERSON: Hello, Inspector!

FORD: I couldn't make Mrs Williams hear, and the downstairs door was open, so I thought –

HENDERSON: (*Pleasantly*) That's all right! Come along in! I'm delighted to see you. As a matter of fact, I've got some good news for you, Inspector.

FORD: Really, sir?

HENDERSON: Yes, I was talking to the Head this morning. He was awfully nice about Roger. He suggests we put him up next term, probably into Four A.

FORD: Four A?

HENDERSON: Yes. That means he'll drop Latin and concentrate more on Maths. I really think that boy of yours has a flair for Maths. I really do.

FORD doesn't react to this news as HENDERSON expected him to.

HENDERSON: Well, I hope your son's more impressed by the news than you are, Inspector.

FORD: (*Quietly*) I'm sorry, but I didn't come here to talk about my son, sir.

HENDERSON: No?

FORD: (*Shaking his head*) No.

HENDERSON: Well, what did you come to talk about?

FORD: (*After a moment, a little more friendly*) May I sit down?

HENDERSON: Yes, of course. (*Almost a sudden thought*) Would you like a glass of sherry? I've an excellent …

HENDERSON crosses to a small table with a decanter on it.

FORD: No, thank you.

FORD sits in the armchair.

HENDERSON:	(*Looking at FORD*) You look worried – depressed. Is anything the matter?
FORD:	Yes, sir.
HENDERSON:	Well, what is it?
FORD:	I've always regarded you as a friend of mine, Mr Henderson. Indeed, since my wife died, you've been a very good friend.
HENDERSON:	It's nice of you to say that, Inspector. But what I did for you and Roger, I'd have done for anyone under the circumstances. You don't owe me anything, if that's what you're thinking.
FORD:	That's what I was thinking, sir.
HENDERSON:	Well, don't. What's this all about?
FORD:	(*After a slight pause*) I'm afraid I've got to ask you some questions, sir. I hope you don't mind.
HENDERSON:	(*Smiling*) Go ahead, if it'll make you any happier.
FORD:	Two days ago when I called to see you I asked you about a man called Rocello.
HENDERSON:	That's right.
FORD:	You said you'd never heard of him.
HENDERSON:	I hadn't.
FORD:	Since I saw you, we've discovered one or two interesting facts about Mr Rocello.
HENDERSON:	Indeed?
FORD:	Yes. Apparently he's well known in Italy – comes from a very distinguished family.
HENDERSON:	(*Shaking his head*) I'd never heard of him.
FORD:	So you said, sir. Mr Henderson, why didn't you tell me you were in Medlow that

24

	afternoon? That you actually visited the houseboat.
HENDERSON:	You didn't ask me.
FORD:	But we discussed the murder, sir. You asked me questions about it. I gave you the details.
HENDERSON:	You told me what I already knew; what I'd read in the newspapers.
FORD:	Yes, I appreciate that, but you should have told me what <u>you</u> knew, sir. You should have told me about your visit to the houseboat. I'm sure there's a simple explanation, Mr Henderson, but you should have told me about it at the time.
HENDERSON:	What makes you think I did visit the houseboat?
FORD:	Someone saw you.
HENDERSON:	The girl you mentioned – Miss Walters? (*Shaking his head, unperturbed*) She made a mistake.
FORD:	(*Watching HENDERSON; quietly*) She doesn't strike me as being the sort of person who would make a mistake, sir.
HENDERSON:	(*Holding the decanter, smiling, still unperturbed*) We all make mistakes, Inspector, even the cleverest of us.
FORD:	Look, Mr Henderson, was Rocello a friend of yours? Did you visit the houseboat?
HENDERSON:	(*Shaking his head*) No. I've told you I'd never heard of Rocello.
FORD:	But you did go into Medlow?
HENDERSON:	(*Quietly, after a moment's consideration*) Yes, I did. I went to buy some books and get my hair cut.

FORD:	Where did you get your hair cut, sir? At Taylor's?
HENDERSON:	Er – yes.
FORD:	(*Shaking his head*) You didn't go to Taylor's sir.
HENDERSON:	(*Unperturbed*) Oh, didn't I? Then it must have been somewhere else. I know I did go to Taylor's one day because –
FORD:	(*Interrupting HENDERSON*) Look, Mr Henderson, let's be perfectly frank with each other.
HENDERSON:	By all means, Inspector.
FORD:	When Miss Walters told me she'd seen you near High Tor, the houseboat, I made enquiries. I discovered that you didn't actually take your car into Medlow but that you parked it in a field about a quarter of a mile from the houseboat.
HENDERSON:	(*After a momentary hesitation*) Was I that near the houseboat? I didn't realise that. Anyway, you're quite right, Inspector, I had a spot of trouble with the car so I parked it and walked the rest of the way.
FORD:	By the rest of the way – you mean you walked into Medlow?
HENDERSON:	Yes, that's right.
FORD:	I find that difficult to believe, sir. You see, I made enquiries at Medlow – I made enquiries at the library – the post office – the picture house – most of the shops and both garages. No one saw you.
HENDERSON:	(*Politely*) No one?
FORD:	(*Shaking his head; seriously*) No one.

FORD rises.

HENDERSON:	Not even Miss Walters –?
FORD:	Miss Walters saw you leaving the houseboat, sir.
HENDERSON:	I respectfully suggest, Inspector, that Miss Walters didn't see anything of the sort. She either imagined it or she needs spectacles.
FORD:	(*Quietly*) I don't think she imagined it, sir. (*He looks straight at HENDERSON*) We'll find out if she needs spectacles. Goodnight, Henderson.
HENDERSON:	(*Pleasantly, smiling*) Goodnight, Inspector.

FORD turns and crosses to the door.

HENDERSON:	Don't forget Tuesday morning, seven o'clock.
FORD:	(*Still serious, unamused*) I shall be here.

FORD goes out. HENDERSON looks towards the door, then turns towards the decanter of sherry. He is about to pour himself a glass of sherry when the telephone rings. He slowly puts down the decanter and crosses to the telephone. He puts his hand on the telephone, hesitates, then lifts the receiver.

HENDERSON:	(*On telephone*) Hello?
COOPER:	(*On the other end*) Is that you, Henderson?
HENDERSON:	Yes.
COOPER:	This is Cooper.
HENDERSON:	Oh, just a moment, Cooper, please.

HENDERSON puts the receiver down on the table, and crosses to the door. He goes out through the door, then returns a few moments later, locking the door behind him. He picks up the receiver.

HENDERSON:	(*On the telephone*) Hello?
COOPER:	Are you alone?
HENDERSON:	Yes, but I've had a visitor. I wanted to make sure he'd gone. It's all right, you can talk.

COOPER:	(*Quietly; yet a note of urgency in his voice*) Henderson, listen – I've got to see you. It's very important.
HENDERSON:	Why, what's happened?
COOPER:	I'll tell you when I see you.
HENDERSON:	Well, where are you? Where are you speaking from?
COOPER:	I'm in a callbox on the Oxford Road, about two miles from Stokenchurch.
HENDERSON:	This is very awkward, Cooper – my car's in dock and I daren't borrow another one in case …
COOPER:	(*Interrupting*) Where's your housekeeper – is she in bed?
HENDERSON:	No, she's in London. She won't be back until tomorrow morning.

A slight pause.

| COOPER: | All right. I'll be with you in fifteen minutes. (*He replaces the receiver*) |

HENDERSON looks at the receiver, slowly replacing it.

| CUT TO: | HENDERSON's study. |

HENDERSON is standing by the window, a glass of sherry in his hand. There is the sound of a car and the reflection from the headlights flicker across the window. He crosses, unlocks the door, and then opens it. He returns to his chair behind the desk and sits watching the open door. After a moment, JAMES COOPER enters. He is a serious looking man in his early fifties.

COOPER:	(*Closing the door behind him*) I'm sorry about this, but it's important.
HENDERSON:	I thought you were going to Liverpool?
COOPER:	I've been. I drove back to Town this morning.
HENDERSON:	It sounds as if you've had quite a day. Would you like a drink?

COOPER:	Yes. I would rather. (*He nods towards the small table*) May I help myself?
HENDERSON:	(*Nodding*) Go ahead.

HENDERSON watches COOPER as he crosses to the small table and mixes himself a drink.

HENDERSON:	Before you tell me what it is you want to see me about, I've got some news for you.
COOPER:	(*Turning*) Yes?
HENDERSON:	Someone saw me on Thursday afternoon; they saw me leaving the houseboat.
COOPER:	How do you know?
HENDERSON:	I've had the local Inspector here; he's been asking questions.

COOPER turns from the table.

COOPER:	Who saw you?
HENDERSON:	A girl – apparently she was on the river.
COOPER:	(*Softly; faintly annoyed*) Blast!
HENDERSON:	Yes, it rather complicates things, doesn't it?
COOPER:	Who was this girl – do you know?
HENDERSON:	Her name's Walters.

COOPER looks at HENDERSON, obviously surprised. He puts the glass down on the table.

COOPER:	Walters? Katherine Walters?
HENDERSON:	(*Curious*) Yes, I believe her name's Katherine.
COOPER:	She's staying with a Dr Sheldon?
HENDERSON:	(*Surprised*) That's right.
COOPER:	But that's why I came down here; that's what I wanted to see you about!
HENDERSON:	(*Puzzled*) I don't understand.
COOPER:	Have you met this girl?
HENDERSON:	No, of course I haven't met her. I know Sheldon, of course, he's my doctor. (*Curious*) But why are you interested in Miss Walters?

29

COOPER: (*A   moment;   significantly;   watching
               HENDERSON's   reaction*) Two   weeks   ago
               she was in Venice.
HENDERSON: In Venice?
COOPER: (*Nodding*) Yes.
HENDERSON: Well, that's a coincidence!
COOPER: (*Quietly*) Is it?
COOPER turns and picks up his drink.
HENDERSON: What do you mean?
COOPER: (*Turning again, towards HENDERSON*) Is it
               a coincidence?
HENDERSON looks across at COOPER in surprise.

END OF EPISODE ONE

EPISODE TWO

OPEN TO: DAVID HENDERSON's Study.

HENDERSON is sitting at his desk. JAMES COOPER is standing looking at him.

HENDERSON: But why are you interested in Miss Walters?

COOPER: (*A moment; significantly*) Two weeks ago she was in Venice.

HENDERSON: In Venice?

COOPER: (*Nodding*) Yes.

HENDERSON: Well, that's a coincidence!

COOPER: (*Quietly*) Is it?

COOPER turns and picks up his drink.

HENDERSON: What do you mean?

COOPER: (*Turning again, towards HENDERSON*) Is it a coincidence?

HENDERSON comes from behind the desk.

HENDERSON: (*Curious*) Cooper, what do you know about this girl?

COOPER: (*Quietly; smiling*) We know that she was in Venice two weeks ago.

HENDERSON: Yes – but what else do you know about her?

COOPER ignores the question; sips his drink.

COOPER: You say she saw you leaving the houseboat on Thursday afternoon?

HENDERSON: Yes. She told the local Inspector; a man called Ford. He's by way of being a friend of mine.

COOPER: Was it Ford that questioned you?

HENDERSON: Yes, it was.

COOPER: Miss Walters must have recognised you.

HENDERSON: (*Nodding; a shade irritated*) Apparently.

COOPER: Would you recognise Miss Walters if you saw her?

HENDERSON: No, of course not. So far as I know I've never even seen the girl.

COOPER looks at HENDERSON; he stands by the small table holding his drink.

COOPER: What sort of a man is her uncle – Dr Sheldon?

HENDERSON: Quite pleasant; bit of an old woman at times.

COOPER: You say he's your doctor?

HENDERSON: Yes.

COOPER: When did you see him last?

HENDERSON: About a month ago. I had trouble with my shoulder.

COOPER sips his drink again.

COOPER: (*After a pause*) I suggest you go on having trouble with it.

HENDERSON: (*Puzzled; faintly irritated*) What do you mean?

COOPER: (*Seriously*) We'd like you to keep an eye on Miss Walters.

COOPER looks at HENDERSON and puts his drink down on the table.

CUT TO: The Kitchen of MICHAEL FORD's house at Medlow, Bucks.

It is a fairly large, modern kitchen, complete with an electric cooker, small Frigidaire, cupboards, wooden table and several chairs, including an old comfortable armchair. There are cups, several glasses and a pot of tea on the table.

FORD is standing by the cooker preparing breakfast, He is dressed in flannel trousers and an open shirt. ROGER enters the kitchen, wearing a dressing gown over his pyjamas.

ROGER: What's cooking, Dad?

FORD: (*Turning*) Back to bed, young man! Go on!

ROGER: (*Surprised*) Why? Aren't we having breakfast together?

FORD: No, you're having it in bed. Go on, it's nearly ready.

ROGER: Can't I have breakfast with you, Dad? I don't
                   like having it in bed, I always spill something.
FORD: I'm expecting Sergeant Broderick. You've
                   got to have your breakfast in bed this
                   morning, Roger. Now don't grumble, there's
                   a good chap.

The doorbell rings.

ROGER: (*Turning*) Oh, all right.
FORD: (*Picking up a plate*) If that's the front door,
                   answer it.

*ROGER goes out. FORD transfers the breakfast from the cooker
to the plate he is holding, then he crosses to the table and pours
out a glass of milk. ROGER returns with DETECTIVE
SERGEANT BRODERICK.*

ROGER: It's Sergeant Broderick, Dad.
FORD: (*Turning*) Hello, Bob, come in! (*He hands
                   ROGER the plate and the glass of milk*)
                   Here's your breakfast, Rog. Now run along!

*ROGER gets a knife and fork out of one of the drawers and then
takes the plate and the glass of milk from his father.*

BRODERICK: (*To FORD, indicating ROGER*) He gets
                   bigger every time I see him.
FORD: Yes, he's grown a lot since he's been at
                   Buckingham.
BRODERICK: How long are you home for, Roger?
ROGER: Eight weeks.
BRODERICK: Eight weeks! Good heavens! (*To FORD*) We
                   missed the bus, Mike. We ought to have been
                   schoolmasters.
FORD: I'm not so sure about that. (*Points to ROGER*)
                   There are times when he takes a bit of
                   handling. I shudder to think what I'd do with
                   forty of 'em.
ROGER: There are sixty boys in our house, Dad.

35

BRODERICK: (*To FORD, smiling*) That must be a headache.

ROGER: Mr Henderson says if it wasn't for the fact that half of us –

FORD: (*Interrupting, dismissing ROGER*) Yes, all right, Roger. Go and have your breakfast before it gets cold, there's a good chap.

ROGER goes out.

BRODERICK: (*To FORD*) He's a nice boy, Mike.

FORD: (*Pointing to a cup of tea*) Yes, Rog is all right.

FORD gives BRODERICK the cup of tea.

BRODERICK: (*Taking the cup of tea*) Thanks. (*He stirs his tea, nodding towards the door*) Does he like Henderson?

FORD: Good heavens, yes! He thinks the sun shines out of him, I'd never have got into Buckingham, you know, if it hadn't been for Henderson.

BRODERICK: I realise that.

FORD: Bob, this Henderson business is worrying the life out of me. It was supposed to be my day off yesterday. I spent ten hours questioning people, hanging about pubs.

BRODERICK nods; stirs his tea some more.

BRODERICK: Yes, I know. (*After a moment; quietly*) Mike, do you know a girl called Billie Reynolds?

FORD: (*Looking up*) Billie Reynolds?

BRODERICK: Yes. She's got a houseboat called Shangri La. It's about two hundred yards from Cooper's place.

FORD: I know the girl you mean. She's a flash-piece.

BRODERICK: (*Laughing*) That's putting it mildly.

FORD: (*Nodding*) Morgan questioned her quite early on. She was out of town when the murder

36

	happened. I checked her story. She caught the 9.25 to London on Wednesday morning. Old Fred down at the station remembers her. He carried her suitcase.
BRODERICK:	(*Thoughtfully*) Yes, I know.
FORD:	Why? Have you seen Billie Reynolds?
BRODERICK:	Yes, I saw her last night. She was in the Rose and Crown at Maidenhead. I bought her a drink. As a matter of fact, I bought her three drinks.
FORD:	Well?
BRODERICK:	I asked her about Cooper and Rocello. She said she knew Cooper by sight, but she'd never seen the Italian. She told me the same as Morgan. She said she left Medlow on Wednesday and returned on Friday night.
FORD:	(*Interested*) Don't you believe her?
BRODERICK:	Yes, I believe her. In any case you say you checked her story.
FORD:	(*Nodding*) Yes, I did. It's perfectly all right.
BRODERICK:	Well, there you are then.

BRODERICK drinks his tea. FORD looks at him for a moment.

FORD:	(*A pause; quietly*) Bob, is there a doubt in your mind about the Reynolds girl?
BRODERICK:	No. No, you wouldn't call it a doubt.
FORD:	Well, what would you call it?

BRODERICK hesitates, then puts down his cup of tea.

BRODERICK:	I find it difficult to believe that she didn't notice Rocello. I accept the fact that she was away when the murder happened, but – well, let's face it, Rocello was down here for nearly a fortnight. Billie must have noticed him.
FORD:	(*Thoughtfully*) Yes, I'm inclined to agree.

BRODERICK: Mike, let's take a look at the facts in this case: An Italian called Paul Rocello is found murdered in one of the houseboats. The boat belongs to a friend of his, a man called Cooper. Cooper disappeared. Correct?

FORD: Correct.

BRODERICK: On the afternoon in question, a Miss Katherine Walters saw a car drive up to the houseboat and she saw a man get into it. Later she identified the man as David Henderson, a housemaster at Buckingham College. Correct?

FORD nods.

BRODERICK: Now, in spite of the fact that Henderson says he didn't go near the houseboat, our investigations have established …

FORD: (*A shade irritated*) Henderson went to the houseboat, there's no doubt about that. The point is – why?

BRODERICK: Well, my bet is he went to see Cooper, instead of which he saw the body, became frightened and made a dash for it.

FORD shakes his head unconvinced.

FORD: Then why didn't he tell me about it? I was quite frank with him. I told him exactly what Miss Walters had told me. I think you're wrong, Bob. Henderson knew Rocello all right.

BRODERICK: I'm not saying he didn't know Rocello. I'm simply saying that the Italian was dead when Henderson reached the houseboat.

FORD: (*Faintly exasperated*) Then why doesn't the damn fool come out into the open and tell us about it?

BRODERICK:	Because he's a friend of Cooper's and he doesn't want to get mixed up in anything.
FORD:	Well, at the moment, he's mixed up in a murder case! (*He stirs his tea*)
BRODERICK:	Yes, that's true. When did Rocello first come over here, do you know?
FORD:	About four weeks ago. According to our information he stayed in London for three days and then went up to Liverpool. From Liverpool he came down here.
BRODERICK:	Was Cooper with him in Liverpool?
FORD:	No, I don't think so.

ROGER enters.

BRODERICK:	I've been thinking about that inscription, Mike, the one that was on the watch.
FORD:	(*Turning from BRODERICK towards ROGER*) What is it, Roger?
ROGER:	I've spilt some milk, Dad, I want a cloth.
FORD:	(*Nodding towards the cupboard*) There's one in the cupboard.

ROGER crosses to the cupboard and takes out a cloth.

FORD:	(*To BRODERICK*) Sorry, Bob, what were you saying?
BRODERICK:	I was saying, I've been thinking about that inscription – the one that was on the watch. What was it? Suavito in modo …
FORD:	… Fortito in re.
ROGER:	(*Looking up*) Gentle in the manner, but vigorous in the deed.
FORD:	(*Surprised, looking at ROGER*) Yes, that's right, Roger.
BRODERICK:	(*Laughing, to FORD*) I tell you, Mike, we'll be working for him before we know where we are.

FORD: (*To ROGER, seriously*) I thought you were very bad at Latin?

ROGER: (*Crossing from the cupboard*) I am. But I remember that quotation because I asked Mr Henderson about it.

FORD: When?

ROGER: Oh, two or three days ago.

FORD: What made you ask Mr Henderson about that particular quotation?

ROGER: It was written on the flyleaf of a book I was reading, and I didn't know what it meant.

BRODERICK: (*Quietly*) What was the book, Roger?

ROGER: It was a book on the Italian Lakes. Mr Henderson lent it to me.

FORD: Was it Mr Henderson's handwriting?

ROGER: Yes, I think so.

BRODERICK: (*Pleasantly*) Have you still got the book, Roger?

ROGER: Yes, I'm still reading it.

The doorbell rings.

FORD: (*Dismissing ROGER*) All right, finish your breakfast. And see who that is, it's probably the post.

ROGER: Yes, all right, Dad.

ROGER goes out.

BRODERICK: (*Quietly*) What do you make of that?

FORD: (*Thoughtfully*) I don't know.

BRODERICK: Is it a coincidence?

FORD: No, no, it can't be. (*He looks at BRODERICK*) Do you still think it was Cooper that Henderson went to see? (*Shaking his head*) There was some tie-up, some connection between Henderson and the Italian, I'm sure of that.

BRODERICK: Yes, it's beginning to look like it. (*He looks at FORD and hesitates*) Mike, why don't you have a serious talk with Henderson?

FORD: I have had a serious talk with him.

BRODERICK: No, I don't mean that. You know what I mean, off the record.

FORD: (*A shade irritated*) I'm not his lawyer, if he needs that kind of advice …

BRODERICK: Look, Mike, you're a friend of his. Once we know what this is all about we might be able to help him.

ROGER enters.

FORD: What is it, Roger?

ROGER: There's a Mr Merson, Dad. He wants to know if you can spare him a few minutes.

RALPH MERSON comes into the kitchen. He is a tall, faintly pedantic man, in his late forties. He is surprised to see BRODERICK.

MERSON: May I come in?

BRODERICK: (*Quietly*) Good morning, Mr Merson.

MERSON: Oh, hello, Sergeant. (*To FORD*) I'm sorry to disturb you at this unearthly hour, Inspector, but I'm catching the eight-ten and I did rather … (*He looks at BRODERICK*) want to have a word with you.

ROGER looks at his father and then goes out.

FORD: What is it you want to see me about?

MERSON looks at BRODERICK again.

BRODERICK: (*To FORD, with the suggestion of a smile*) I'm afraid Mrs Merson's in trouble. She parked her car in front of the Fire Station, and unfortunately …

MERSON: (*Interrupting*) No, that's not why I'm here, Sergeant. I wouldn't dream of troubling the

	Inspector over a little thing like that. (*He looks at BRODERICK*) This is a personal matter.
BRODERICK:	Oh. Oh, well in that case … (*To FORD*) I'll see you later, Mike.
FORD:	Yes, all right, Bob.

BRODERICK crosses towards the door, followed by FORD.

BRODERICK:	It's all right, I can let myself out.

BRODERICK goes out. FORD turns towards MERSON.

FORD:	Well, Mr Merson?
MERSON:	I don't think we've actually met before, have we, Inspector?
FORD:	No, I don't think we have, sir.
MERSON:	(*Nervously, obviously worried*) I live at Seldon House, Waverley Avenue. It's the large house with the tennis court, on the corner of …
FORD:	(*Unhelpful*) Yes, I know. (*Quietly*) What is it you want to see me about?
MERSON:	About – about this murder. The Italian chap…
FORD:	(*Quite surprised*) Go on, Mr Merson …

MERSON hesitates, he is obviously ill at ease.

MERSON:	Inspector, I'll be perfectly frank with you. I'm in rather a spot. I saw something on Wednesday night – or rather Thursday morning – that I think you ought to know about. On the other hand I don't want you, or anyone else – my wife for instance – to think that … (*He hesitates*)

FORD crosses and closes the door.

FORD:	(*Turning*) You can be quite frank with me, Mr Merson. If this matter doesn't concern your wife there's no reason why she should know anything about it.

MERSON: Yes, well, the point is Mrs Merson's away at the moment; she's staying with her sister in Edinburgh, so I ...

FORD: Spent last Wednesday night with a friend – is that it?

MERSON: (*Grateful for FORD's assistance*) Yes. Yes, that's right, Inspector.

FORD: (*Quietly*) Go on, sir.

MERSON: This – friend of mine's rather good at Canasta, and it's a game I'm particularly fond of.

FORD: I see, sir.

MERSON: Mrs Merson doesn't like cards, she won't even have a pack in the house, so naturally I – er – take every opportunity of ...

FORD: I understand, sir.

MERSON: Well, my friend has a houseboat called Shangri La, it's not very far from the one where ...

FORD: (*Surprised; interrupting MERSON*) Shangri La?

MERSON: Yes.

FORD: Then you're talking about Miss Reynolds – Billie Reynolds?

MERSON: (*Embarrassed*) Yes, that's right. Do you know her. Inspector?

FORD: Yes, I know her, but – I thought Miss Reynolds was in London on Wednesday night.

MERSON: No, she went up to London – she caught the 9.25 in the morning – but she didn't stay there. I – brought her back to Medlow.

FORD: Oh, I'm beginning to understand. The trip to London was just to give people the impression that Miss Reynolds was away for two or three days.

MERSON: (*Interrupting, with a little laugh*) Well, you know what the local people are, Inspector. One can't be

	too careful. Mark you, not that there's anything for them to be …
FORD:	(*Interrupting MERSON*) Go on, Mr Merson.
MERSON:	I spent Wednesday night with Billie – Miss Reynolds – playing Canasta and at about half past two in the morning we went up on deck. To be perfectly frank it was rather a hot night and …
FORD:	(*Nodding*) And you felt like a breath of fresh air.
MERSON:	Exactly. Well, we'd been on deck about five minutes when a car suddenly appeared and stopped opposite Cooper's place. What do they call the houseboat – High – something or other?
FORD:	High Tor.
MERSON:	That's it. Two men got out of the car and they lifted a third man from the back seat and carried him on the boat. It was the Italian chap.
FORD:	Are you sure?
MERSON:	Yes, I'm positive. I recognised him immediately. Naturally, we thought they'd been on a binge and the Italian was drunk. That's what it looked like.
FORD:	Did you recognise either of the two men?
MERSON:	No.
FORD:	Did Miss Reynolds?
MERSON:	(*Hesitantly*) Well, I asked her and she said she didn't, but I rather got the impression that she had seen one of them before.
FORD:	What gave you that impression?
MERSON:	Oh, I don't know. It was just the way she looked, I suppose.
FORD:	You say, it was you that recognised Rocello?
MERSON:	Yes. I'd seen him in the village once or twice.
FORD:	(*Thoughtfully*) And this happened on Thursday morning at about …
MERSON:	About half past two.

FORD: Mr Merson, tell me, do you think the two men saw you, by any chance?

MERSON: I doubt it.

FORD: Wasn't there a light showing?

MERSON: Er – no, I'm afraid not. We were not particularly anxious to draw attention to ourselves.

FORD: (*Quietly*) I see.

MERSON: I – I hope I've done the right thing in telling you all this, Inspector.

FORD: You certainly have, Mr Merson.

MERSON: You see, after I read about the murder it suddenly occurred to me that perhaps Rocello wasn't drunk after all – perhaps he'd already been murdered and the men we saw were simply bringing him – the body, that is – back to the houseboat.

FORD doesn't answer; he looks thoughtful.

MERSON: After all, it's possible isn't it?

FORD: (*Thoughtfully*) It is indeed. (*Looking at him*) Does Miss Reynolds know you've come to see me?

MERSON: Good heavens, no! No one knows. (*Faintly alarmed*) Look, Inspector, I've been perfectly frank with you about all this. I needn't have told you anything about …

FORD rises and holds out his hand, he is virtually dismissing MERSON.

FORD: You've been very frank, sir, and I appreciate it. Now don't worry. (*Shaking his head*) We're not interested in your private life, Mr Merson.

MERSON: Now for heavens sake don't get the wrong impression, Inspector.

FORD: I don't think I've got the wrong impression, sir. (*Looks at his watch*) Did you say you were catching the eight ten?

MERSON: Yes. (*Takes his watch from his inside pocket and glances at it*) My goodness, yes! I must get a move on!

FORD: I'll see you out, sir.

FORD goes out with MERSON.

The camera slowly tracks in to a cup on the kitchen table.

CUT TO: *A close-up of another cup on another table. The spout of a teapot appears and tea is poured into the cup. The camera tracks back to reveal BILLIE REYNOLDS in the main cabin of Shangri La. The cabin is a little over furnished and, like BILLIE herself, a shade too exotic. BILLIE is wearing a negligée and is irritatingly attractive in a common way. She puts four spoonfuls of sugar into the cup, adds milk, and then crosses over to the settee. She surrounds herself with cushions and is just making herself comfy when the doorbell rings.*

BILLIE: (*Looking up; annoyed*) Who is it?

FORD's VOICE: Inspector Ford.

The door opens and FORD looks into the cabin.

FORD: May I come in?

BILLIE: It looks as if you are in!

FORD enters, closing the door behind him.

FORD: (*Pleasantly*) I'm sorry if I've interrupted your breakfast.

BILLIE: It's been done before, duckie. What is it you want?

FORD: Well, I'd like to have a chat with you, Miss Reynolds, if it's convenient?

BILLIE: What if it isn't convenient?

FORD: Then I'll come back some other time.

BILLIE looks at FORD; she rather likes what she sees.

BILLIE: What is it you want to chat about – the weather?

FORD: No. You.

BILLIE: (*Surprised*) Me? What d'you mean – me?

46

FORD: (*Looking down at BILLIE; smiling*) You, Miss
            Reynolds. You may not know it, but you're quite a
            personality in these parts.
BILLIE: Look – is this an official visit?
FORD: More or less.
BILLIE: Then keep your mind on the job, copper.
FORD: (*Smiling*) Billie, I want you to tell me … By the
            way, do you mind if I call you Billie?
BILLIE: Go ahead, Mike. It is Mike, isn't it?
FORD: (*Amused*) Yes, it's Mike.
BILLIE: Well, go ahead, Mike, but be careful – your third
            degree's showing.

FORD grins and sits down on the chair opposite the settee.

FORD: How long have you know Ralph Merson?
BILLIE: About a year. He visits me twice a month. He pays
            me a fiver a week, he's got a duodenal ulcer, he
            once did a hole in one and he can't play canasta for
            toffee.
FORD: Well, that seems to take care of Mr Merson.
BILLIE: There are a few other details. He takes me off his
            income tax, his wife doesn't understand him and
            beneath a cold exterior beats a heart of gold – well,
            rolled gold, anyway.
FORD: Mr Merson doesn't sound very original.
BILLIE: (*Amused*) You'd be surprised. (*Nods to the table*)
            Reach me the cigarettes, duckie.

*FORD takes out his own cigarette case and offers BILLIE one.
She looks at him and takes a cigarette. FORD replaces his case
and produces a lighter. BILLIE accepts the light.*

FORD: (*Replacing his lighter*) What happened on Thursday
            morning?
BILLIE: What part of Thursday morning?

FORD: You know what I mean, Billie. You and Merson saw the Italian; you saw two men bring him back to the houseboat.

BILLIE: Did we?

FORD: Yes.

BILLIE smokes his cigarette.

BILLIE: I don't remember.

FORD: (*Shaking his head*) You remember all right. Merson says you recognised one of the men.

BILLIE: (*Annoyed*) I didn't recognise anyone. It was Ralph that … (*She stops*)

FORD: (*Quietly*) It was Ralph that what?

BILLIE: It was Ralph that recognised Morello or Rocello or whatever his name was. I'd never seen him before.

FORD: (*Almost a note of sarcasm*) Well, if you'd never seen him before – what was your first impression?

BILLIE: What d'you mean?

FORD: Did you think he was drunk?

BILLIE: Yes, of course I did. He was as tight as an owl. He couldn't stand up. His friends had to carry him.

FORD: Who were his friends?

BILLIE: I've told you, I don't know. I didn't recognise them. I'd never seen them before.

FORD: (*Leaning forward*) Billie, I'm going to ask you a question. I want the truth.

BILLIE: Sure. I'm telling you the truth.

FORD: Do you know a man called Henderson – David Henderson?

BILLIE: (*Unhesitatingly*) Yes, he's a housemaster at Buckingham College.

FORD: (*Faintly surprised*) That's right. Was he one of the men?

BILLIE: Of course he wasn't! If he had have been I should have recognised him.

BILLIE rises; stubs out her cigarette on the ashtray on the table.

FORD: (*Watching BILLIE*) When did you meet Henderson?

BILLIE: About a year ago.

FORD: Where?

BILLIE: (*Turning; with heavy sarcasm*) The head boy threw a cocktail party.

FORD: (*Patiently*) Where did you meet him, Billie?

BILLIE: Some of the Buckingham boys used to swim down here and – well, I used to pop in occasionally. (*FORD gives her a look*) Well, why not for Gawd's sake, it used to liven things up.

FORD: Go on …

BILLIE: The School didn't like it. They wrote me a letter and asked me to "kindly refrain from bathing while the boys were taking exercise". You can imagine how that went down. I bought a bikini.

FORD: Go on, Billie.

BILLIE: Well, after two letters they sent Henderson to see me. The saucy devil said I was undermining morale. Me! Undermining morale, for Pete's sake.

FORD: What happened?

BILLIE: (*Faintly irritated*) Oh, the boys don't swim in the river anymore, that's all. It's out of bounds.

FORD: Have you seen Henderson since?

BILLIE: Once; in the village. (*Laughing*) I damn nearly gave him the V sign. (*She picks up the teapot*) Would you like a cup of tea?

FORD: No, thank you, Billie. I must be off. Some other time.

FORD crosses to the door.

BILLIE: (*Looking at him; smiling*) Well, you know where to find me.

FORD turns; smiles at BILLIE and goes out. BILLIE's expression changes slightly, it is a shade harder.

CUT TO: The Living Room of DR SHELDON's house.

DAVID HENDERSON enters from the consulting room, followed by SHELDON. The DOCTOR is assisting HENDERSON with his jacket. It is obvious that SHELDON has been examining HENDERSON's shoulder.

SHELDON: (*As he enters*) It's an awful nuisance, I agree – but you've really nothing to worry about.

HENDERSON: I wouldn't mind so much if it didn't interfere with my tennis.

SHELDON: Well, you try the ointment I've suggested. It's not a miracle worker, but I think it'll make a difference.

HENDERSON: One of my colleagues suggested an osteopath. Is that a good idea?

SHELDON: We'll try the ointment first.

KATHERINE enters from the hall; she hesitates on seeing HENDERSON and the DOCTOR.

KATHERINE: Oh, I'm sorry, I thought you were …

SHELDON: That's all right, my dear. Come along in! (*To HENDERSON*) I don't think you've met my niece. Miss Walters.

HENDERSON: (*Pleasantly; shaking hands*) How do you do, Miss Walters?

SHELDON: (*To KATHERINE*) This is Mr Henderson, Katherine. (*He looks at her*) He's a housemaster at Buckingham College.

HENDERSON: (*Smiling*) For my sins …

KATHERINE: (*Hesitantly; a shade embarrassed*) It looks a very nice school …

HENDERSON: Have you seen it?

KATHERINE: Yes, I – drove up there the other morning with my uncle.

50

HENDERSON: It's really very pleasant; one mustn't grumble. How long are you staying in Medlow, Miss Walters?

KATHERINE: I'm not really sure, probably another week or so.

HENDERSON: Do you play tennis?

KATHERINE: Er – yes, I do.

HENDERSON: Well, why not drive up to the school one day and have a game with me?

KATHERINE: (*A little taken aback*) Thank you very much.

HENDERSON: It's very agreeable at the moment, the boys are on holiday.

There is a slight pause.

SHELDON: (*Making conversation*) I don't think you've played since you've been down here, have you, Katherine?

KATHERINE: No, the last game I had was in Rome about two months ago.

HENDERSON: (*Politely interested*) Oh – you've been abroad then, Miss Walters?

KATHERINE: Yes; I've been in Italy for two or three months.

HENDERSON: On holiday?

KATHERINE: No, I'm a dress designer. I've been working for one of the Italian fashion houses.

HENDERSON: And very nice too! (*To SHELDON*) Now why didn't I think of that?

KATHERINE: (*Watching HENDERSON*) Do you know Italy, Mr Henderson?

HENDERSON: Yes, I do, quite well. I was there during the war. (*To SHELDON; apparently a sudden thought*) I say, this murder's an extraordinary business, isn't it? The Italian chap, I mean.

SHELDON: Yes, it is indeed.

HENDERSON:	(*To SHELDON*) It's been very embarrassing for me. Someone – I can't imagine who – told the police they'd seen me visiting the houseboat.
SHELDON:	Er – the houseboat?
HENDERSON:	Yes, the one where the murder was committed.
KATHERINE:	And did you?
HENDERSON:	(*Turning; politely*) Did I what?
KATHERINE:	Visit the houseboat?
HENDERSON:	Good Lord, no! Of course not. I'd never even heard of the fellow. What was his name – Rocello or something?
SHELDON:	Paul Rocello.
HENDERSON:	That's right. Paul Rocello. I don't think I ever saw him. Unless I saw him in the village without realising it. The Inspector said he was from Venice.

JUDY enters.

JUDY:	(*To SHELDON*) Excuse me, sir.
SHELDON:	Yes, what is it, Judy?
JUDY:	A Mr Craven would like to see you, sir.
SHELDON:	Oh, yes, of course.

JUDY waits.

HENDERSON:	Have you ever been to Venice, Miss Walters?
KATHERINE:	Yes, I was there a fortnight ago.
SHELDON:	(*To KATHERINE, faintly surprised*) Were you. Katherine? I didn't know that.
KATHERINE:	Yes. I broke my journey there. I didn't want to leave Italy without seeing Venice.
HENDERSON:	I can understand that. (*Suddenly; pleasantly*) Well, if you ever feel like a game of tennis, Miss Walters, give me a ring.
KATHERINE:	Thank you.

HENDERSON: Your uncle's got my phone number.

SHELDON crosses to the door with HENDERSON.

SHELDON: You've got the prescription I gave you?

HENDERSON: Yes, thank you, doctor.

SHELDON: (*To JUDY*) Ask Mr Craven to come in, Judy.

JUDY: Yes, sir.

SHELDON: (*To HENDERSON*) Let me know how you get on.

HENDERSON nods, smiles at KATHERINE and goes out with JUDY. SHELDON returns to KATHERINE.

SHELDON: Well – what do you think of him?

KATHERINE: (*Hesitantly*) He seems a nice enough person. A little different from what I expected.

SHELDON: What did you expect?

KATHERINE: I don't know. Someone not quite so sure of themselves.

SHELDON: Are you still sure of yourself, Katherine?

KATHERINE: What do you mean?

SHELDON: Was it Henderson you saw?

KATHERINE: (*Quietly; yet positively*) Yes. (*Nodding*) It was Henderson.

SHELDON takes out his pipe and tobacco pouch. KATHERINE crosses and takes a book from the bookshelf.

KATHERINE: Do you mind if I borrow this?

SHELDON: No, of course not. But don't go, Katherine. I want you to meet young Craven.

KATHERINE: (*Turning*) Who's young Craven?

SHELDON: He's the son of a patient of mine. He telephoned me this morning and said he wanted to meet you.

KATHERINE: Why should he want to meet me?

SHELDON: He's a journalist. I think he wants to do an article for the local rag.

KATHERINE: On me?

SHELDON: No, I imagine on your job. What the smart
              Italian girl wears for breakfast, that sort of
              thing.
KATHERINE: Oh.
SHELDON: Robin's a queer bird; clever, but he doesn't
              seem to get anywhere. He wrote a novel about
              three years ago, got awfully good notices.

ROBIN CRAVEN enters. He is an intelligent, but somewhat odd-looking man in his twenties. He wears a bow tie and is neat and fastidious about his dress.

CRAVEN: But no one read it.

SHELDON turns and sees CRAVEN in the doorway.

SHELDON: Oh, hello, Robin! (*Introducing KATHERINE*)
              This is Miss Walters.

CRAVEN peers at KATHERINE through his glasses; crosses and shakes hands with her.

CRAVEN: (*Smiling*) It's nice of you to see me, Miss
              Walters. Very nice. I appreciate it.
SHELDON: Sit down, Robin. Would you like a drink?
CRAVEN: May I have a very small sherry?
SHELDON: Er – yes, certainly. (*Smiling at KATHERINE*)
              Katherine?
KATHERINE: Not for me, thank you.

SHELDON crosses to the drinks cabinet.

SHELDON: How's your mother, Robin?
CRAVEN: She's very well, thank you. Very well –
              considering.

CRAVEN looks at KATHERINE and smiles.
A pause.

KATHERINE: (*Making conversation*) I understand you're
              interested in women's fashions, Mr Craven?
CRAVEN: Women's fashions?
KATHERINE: Yes.
CRAVEN: Not particularly.

54

KATHERINE looks across at SHELDON who is pouring the sherry.

SHELDON: (*To CRAVEN*) I thought you wanted to interview Katherine?

CRAVEN: I do, very much. (*He smiles at KATHERINE*)

KATHERINE: Well, I'm a fashion designer. I'm afraid my opinion isn't worth a great deal on any other subject.

CRAVEN: I wouldn't say that, Miss Walters. I jolly well wouldn't say that.

SHELDON looks at KATHERINE; brings the glass of sherry to CRAVEN.

SHELDON: (*To CRAVEN*) Here's your sherry.

CRAVEN: Oh, thank you, sir.

CRAVEN sips his sherry; looks at KATHERINE and SHELDON.

KATHERINE: (*Quietly; a shade suspicious*) What is it you want to see me about?

CRAVEN: (*Quite pleasant; taking KATHERINE by surprise*) I understand you were on the river on Thursday afternoon, the day the murder was committed. Did you see anyone, Miss Walters?

KATHERINE: What makes you think I was on the river?

CRAVEN: You hired a punt from Barker Brothers.

KATHERINE: (*Resenting CRAVEN's manner*) Are you a detective as well as a journalist?

CRAVEN: (*Shaking his head*) Good Lord, no! Everyone to his trade. Although, come to think of it, I'd make an awfully good detective. I've plenty of nerve; tenacity. When I get my teeth into a thing I never let go. I think the doctor will confirm that – won't you, doctor?

SHELDON: Yes. I think you've got tenacity, Robin.

55

KATHERINE:	(*Irritated by CRAVEN*) What have you got your teeth into at the moment, Mr Craven?
CRAVEN:	Why, this murder. The Italian. Paul Rocello. (*To SHELDON*) I've written a fascinating article for The Daily Dispatch. Do you take The Dispatch, doctor?
SHELDON:	Why, yes – but that's a London paper – a National.
CRAVEN:	Of course. I'm their local correspondent.
SHELDON:	Oh, I didn't know that.
CRAVEN:	Neither did I, until last night.
SHELDON:	Oh – congratulations.
CRAVEN:	(*Smiling*) Thank you.
KATHERINE:	What's this article of yours about?
CRAVEN:	Rocello. Paul Rocello.
KATHERINE:	But no one knows anything about Rocello.
CRAVEN:	I do.
KATHERINE:	(*Quietly*) What do you know about him?
CRAVEN:	Well, I know that he was an Italian, that he was born in Venice and that he was a great friend of Count Paragi's.
SHELDON:	Count Paragi? Wasn't he the chap that has something to do with midget submarines?
CRAVEN:	That's right. During the war he commanded a branch of the Italian Marines; they were called the 12th Flotilla. The flotilla consisted of midget submarines and frogmen. (*Smiling*) Paul Rocello was one of the frogmen.
SHELDON:	Are you sure about this?
CRAVEN:	Quite sure. It's all in the article I've written. "Murder of a Frogman" by Robin Craven. That's not my title, by the way.
KATHERINE:	How did you find out all this?

CRAVEN: Well, I'd like to be able to tell you that it was the result of exhaustive inquiries and grim determination, but I'm afraid it wasn't anything of the sort. (*He takes his wallet out of his pocket and extracts a piece of paper*) Someone sent me this note.

SHELDON takes the note from CRAVEN and looks at it. There is a picture of a Frogman's outfit underneath which is written in a legible handwriting: Portrait of R. 1943.

SHELDON: Who sent you this?

KATHERINE takes the note, looks at it, and then returns it to CRAVEN.

CRAVEN: I don't know; it was pushed through my letter box on Tuesday morning, At first I just didn't see the point of it. Then suddenly I remembered that the Italians were pretty hot on this Frogmen business so I went down to the British Museum and did a spot of research. It wasn't long before I realised I was on to something. I sent Count Paragi a cable and he replied by return. Rocello was a Frogman all right. He was hot stuff; Italian gold medallist, and all the rest of it – one of the real underwater boys.

SHELDON: Have you told the police this?

CRAVEN: (*Smiling; shaking his head*) They can read about it in The Daily Dispatch.

SHELDON: I shouldn't like to be in your shoes when they do read about it.

CRAVEN: Why not? I'm a freelance, it's a free country.

SHELDON: Yes, but surely, withholding evidence can be a pretty serious offence.

CRAVEN: (*Putting down his sherry glass*) But I haven't withheld any evidence. All I've done is

	unearth the facts – they could have done that for themselves. (*Turning towards KATHERINE*) Now, if Miss Walters had seen something – or someone – on Thursday afternoon and said nothing to the police about it, that would be a clear case of withholding evidence.
KATHERINE:	I saw nothing on Thursday afternoon that would interest you or the police.
CRAVEN:	Oh. (*A moment; a suggestion of a smile*) But the police did interview you?
KATHERINE:	Naturally. I was on the river.
CRAVEN:	They don't usually interview people without a very good reason, Miss Walters.
KATHERINE:	Really? That's interesting.
CRAVEN:	(*Puzzled*) Interesting?
KATHERINE:	Yes. I have a shrewd suspicion they'll be interviewing you tomorrow morning, Mr Craven.

The smile fades slightly from CRAVEN's face.

CUT TO: DAVID HENDERSON's Study.

BILLIE REYNOLDS is sitting in an armchair; she is sitting opposite the door waiting for HENDERSON. She is wearing her best cocktail dress and wears and carries a number of equally gay accessories. The door opens and HENDERSON returns from his interview with DR SHELDON. He stops when he sees BILLIE.

HENDERSON:	(*Obviously surprised*) Good afternoon.
BILLIE:	Hello, stranger!
HENDERSON:	It's Miss Reynolds, isn't it?
BILLIE:	That's right. Billie Reynolds. You came to see me twelve months ago.
HENDERSON:	Yes, I remember.

58

BILLIE:	Your housekeeper said I could wait in here, I hope you don't mind.
HENDERSON:	No, of course not. What is it you want to see me about?

BILLIE rises and moves across to HENDERSON.

BILLIE:	(*Smiling*) Do you remember the last time we met?
HENDERSON:	I do. I do indeed.
BILLIE:	It wasn't exactly the beginning of a beautiful friendship, was it?
HENDERSON:	(*A suggestion of a smile*) I was under the impression we got on swimmingly together.
BILLIE:	You can say that again!
HENDERSON:	What can I do for you, Miss Reynolds?

BILLIE looks at HENDERSON; stands facing him.

BILLIE:	(*After a moment*) You can give me a cigarette, if you've got one.

HENDERSON hesitates; crosses, picks up a box of cigarettes from the table.

HENDERSON:	(*Offering BILLIE a cigarette*) You could have helped yourself.
BILLIE:	(*Taking a cigarette*) Ladies don't help themselves, Mr Henderson – or perhaps you don't think I'm a lady.

HENDERSON quietly looks BILLIE up and down.

HENDERSON:	(*Quite matter of fact*) Yes; I think you're a lady.

HENDERSON takes out his lighter and lights BILLIE's cigarette. There is a pause.

BILLIE looks at her cigarette.

BILLIE:	I was sorry to hear about your Italian friend.
HENDERSON:	My Italian friend?
BILLIE:	Yes. Rocello, or whatever his name was.

HENDERSON:	(*After a moment*) You're mistaken. He wasn't a friend of mine.
BILLIE:	(*Casually*) Oh, wasn't he, duckie?
HENDERSON:	(*Watching BILLIE*) No.
BILLIE:	Oh, I'm sorry. I thought he was. (*She looks at her cigarette*)
HENDERSON:	What gave you that impression?
BILLIE:	(*Still looking at the cigarette*) M'm?
HENDERSON:	I said: what gave you the impression that Rocello was a friend of mine?
BILLIE:	(*Holding up her cigarette*) I think this has gone out, sweetie, do you mind?

HENDERSON takes out his lighter again; flicks it. He watches BILLIE as she lights her cigarette again.

HENDERSON:	You haven't answered my question – about Rocello?
BILLIE:	I saw you bring him home.
HENDERSON:	(*Puzzled*) When?
BILLIE:	The night he was tight.
HENDERSON:	I'm sorry, but I don't know what you're talking about.
BILLIE:	Yes, you do, duckie. You know perfectly well. You and Cooper brought him home one night, or rather early one morning. He was as drunk as a Lord.

HENDERSON looks at BILLIE; for the very first time since the murder he is apparently perturbed.

HENDERSON:	When was this?
BILLIE:	Last week – the day he was murdered. You dropped him at the houseboat at about two o'clock in the morning. He was that drunk he couldn't even walk; you had to carry him.
HENDERSON:	(*Tensely*) Where were you when this happened?

BILLIE:	Never you mind!
HENDERSON:	(*A shade tense*) Where were you?
BILLIE:	Well, if you must know, I was entertaining a gentleman friend. I do quite a bit of entertaining you know – one way and another.
HENDERSON:	Did your friend recognise Rocello?
BILLIE:	Yes – but not you, sweetie. You needn't worry, he didn't recognise you.
HENDERSON:	(*Quietly; looking at BILLIE*) Have you told anyone else about this?
BILLIE:	No. No, I haven't told anyone else – not yet.
HENDERSON:	What do you mean – not yet.
BILLIE:	Well, I might be tempted to tell them about it, if someone asked me. But no one's asked me, sweetie.
HENDERSON:	(*A moment; looking straight at BILLIE*) What is it you want?
BILLIE:	I don't want anything.
HENDERSON:	(*A shade angry*) Then why are you here?
BILLIE:	My! You are quick off the mark!
HENDERSON:	(*Regretting his remark*) I'm sorry. I didn't mean to be rude.
BILLIE:	I just want to be friends, that's all.
HENDERSON:	(*A moment; quietly*) Well, there's no reason why we shouldn't be friends, Billie.
BILLIE:	(*Looking at HENDERSON; smiling*) You did annoy me last year. I was furious with you.
HENDERSON:	I was only doing my job.
BILLIE:	Yes, I know, but you were so stuffy about it. All that business about undermining morale.
HENDERSON:	It was the Upper Fifth I was thinking of. You didn't undermine my morale.
BILLIE:	(*Pleased; moving nearer to HENDERSON*) Didn't I, sweetie?

61

HENDERSON:	(*Unable to conceal his anxiety*) You haven't told anyone else about this, have you?
BILLIE:	About what?
HENDERSON:	About seeing me and Rocello and …
BILLIE:	No, of course not! I've told you I haven't!
HENDERSON:	You mustn't! You mustn't say a word to anyone – you understand?
BILLIE:	(*Quietly; a sudden thought*) Why not? It wasn't you that murdered …?
HENDERSON:	Good heavens, no; of course not! Put that idea right out of your head. Rocello was a friend of mine.
BILLIE:	Then what are you worried about?
HENDERSON:	Well, I just don't want to be asked a lot of questions, that's all. I'm in a difficult position, Billie. You know what I mean. A housemaster at a public school.
BILLIE:	Yes. I know what you mean, Teacher.

BILLIE turns away from HENDERSON. She looks down at the chess set on the table, after a moment she picks up a Knight.

BILLIE:	(*Turning*) What's this?
HENDERSON:	That? It's a chessman.
BILLIE:	Yes, I know – but what kind?
HENDERSON:	It's a Knight.

BILLIE puts it down and picks up a BISHOP.

BILLIE:	And this?
HENDERSON:	It's a Bishop.
BILLIE:	(*Pointing*) And this?
HENDERSON:	That's a Castle. (*He points to various chessmen*) Bishop, Pawn, Knight, King, Castle …
BILLIE:	My old man used to play chess. The funny old devil used to fall asleep over it. It's a game I've always wanted to learn curiously enough.

HENDERSON: Well, why don't you?
BILLIE: Oh, I dunno. (*Significantly*) I've never had anyone to teach me.
HENDERSON looks at BILLIE for a moment.
HENDERSON: Would you like me to teach you?
BILLIE: Well – (*Looking at HENDERSON; intrigued*) Are you a good teacher, Mr Henderson?
HENDERSON: I've had very few complaints.
BILLIE laughs.

CUT TO: Outside BILLIE REYNOLDS' houseboat Shangri La. It is about eight o'clock in the evening.
HENDERSON walks down the tow path and crosses onto the houseboat. He wears an overcoat and carries a chess board, a small wooden (chess) box and a bottle of champagne.

CUT TO: The interior of the houseboat; the main cabin.
The door opens and HENDERSON pops his head into the cabin.
HENDERSON: (*Calling*) Anybody at home?
BILLIE: (*From an adjoining cabin*) I'll be with you in a moment, duckie.
HENDERSON enters.
HENDERSON: (*Calling*) Do you like champagne?
BILLIE: Yes, please, Teacher!
HENDERSON puts the chess board and box and the bottle of champagne down on the table and then takes off his overcoat and hangs it on the peg on the door.
HENDERSON: (*Calling*) Where do you keep your glasses?
BILLIE: In the corner cupboard!
HENDERSON looks round, sees the cupboard and crosses over to it. He takes out two glasses and then returns to the table. He picks up the champagne bottle and proceeds to open it. As the bottle pops open BILLIE enters from her cabin. She is wearing a less formal dress than in the preceding scene.

63

BILLIE: My! I didn't expect champagne! I thought you were going to teach me chess!

HENDERSON pours out the drinks and hands one to BILLIE.

HENDERSON: (*Looking at BILLIE's dress*) I am. Eventually. (*He raises his glass*) Skoal!

BILLIE: Checkmate! (*She empties her glass*)

HENDERSON laughs.

BILLIE: Is that right – checkmate?

HENDERSON: (*Amused*) That's right. (*He puts his glass – untouched – down on the table and picks up the bottle of champagne*) Have you ever played chess before?

BILLIE: No, never.

HENDERSON: (*Refilling BILLIE's glass*) Do you know anything about it?

BILLIE: No, I haven't a clue. (*She raises her glass to HENDERSON*) But I'll learn, sweetie.

BILLIE drinks; almost emptying her glass again. HENDERSON turns and prepares the chess board and opens the box.

BILLIE: (*Looking at her glass*) My! This stuff certainly goes to your head!

HENDERSON: (*Turning; picking up the bottle of champagne*) Only the first two glasses. (*Filling BILLIE's glass again*) After that …

BILLIE: (*Laughing*) You're floating on air! (*She drinks*)

HENDERSON returns the bottle to the table; takes the chessmen out of the box and starts to place them on the board.

BILLIE: (*Quietly; a shade alarmed*) My God, this stuff is certainly strong … (*She puts her hand out and takes hold of a chair*)

HENDERSON: (*Turning*) Now the first thing you've got to learn about this game … (*He stops; looks at BILLIE*) Are you all right?

64

BILLIE:	I don't know. My head's going round and round and … (*She feels her forehead*) I've never felt quite like this before.
HENDERSON:	It's a bit stuffy down here – would you like to go on deck?
BILLIE:	I don't think so. (*She looks at the glass she is still holding*) This stuff's awfully strong …
HENDERSON:	Is it? It shouldn't be. (*He picks up the bottle and looks at it*) It's Bollinger '45'.
BILLIE:	Well, I've never had champagne that affected me quite like … this … before …

Suddenly the glass drops from BILLIE's hand and she falls forward, knocking several of the chessmen off the table. HENDERSON springs forward and catches her; he holds her in his arms for a moment and then puts her down into the armchair. There is no movement from BILLIE; she is obviously either dead or unconscious.

HENDERSON stands and looks down at BILLIE, his manner tense and serious. Suddenly he picks up the chessmen from the floor and puts them on the table, then he takes a silk handkerchief out of his breast pocket and crosses to the door. He wipes the door handle with the handkerchief and then returns to the table and picks up his untouched glass of champagne. He empties the champagne back into the bottle and then proceeds to wipe his fingerprints off the glass with the silk handkerchief. His manner is grim and determined; he looks down at BILLIE as he cleans the glass.

END OF EPISODE TWO

EPISODE THREE

OPEN TO: The interior of the houseboat; the main cabin.

HENDERSON stands and looks down at BILLIE, his manner tense and serious. Suddenly he takes a silk handkerchief out of his breast pocket and crosses to the door. He wipes the door handle with the handkerchief and then returns to the table and picks up his untouched glass of champagne. He empties the champagne back into the bottle and then proceeds to wipe his fingerprints off the glass with the silk handkerchief. His manner is grim and determined; he looks down at BILLIE as he cleans the glass. Having finally cleaned the glass to his satisfaction HENDERSON crosses and replaces it in the cupboard. He then crosses to his overcoat and takes a torch from one of the pockets. He switches off the light, moves over to the porthole-style-window, throws it open, and begins to signal with the torch.

CUT TO: The Living Room of MICHAEL FORD's house at Medlow. Early Morning.

FORD and ROGER are sitting at the table having their breakfast. There is a newspaper propped up in front of FORD and a book in front of ROGER. They are reading and eating. After a little while ROGER breaks the silence.

ROGER: (*Looking up*) What does parallel longitudinal mean, Dad?

FORD: (*Looking up; surprised*) What does what mean?

ROGER: (*Reading from the book*) Parallel longitudinal.

FORD: Well, it means that – er – that … What on earth is it you're reading?

ROGER: It's the book Mr Henderson lent me. (*Reading*) It says: "The relief of the peninsula is arranged in three parallel longitudinal strips" …

FORD: Yes – well – there you are. It's quite simple. It means that the – er – peninsula is arranged in three parallel … er …

The doorbell starts to ring.

FORD: (*Suddenly, relieved*) That's the doorbell, Rog.
             See who it is.

*ROGER looks at his father; grins, and goes out. FORD leans
across the table, picks up the book, looks at it, scratches his
head, then puts it down as ROGER returns with SERGEANT
BRODERICK. The SERGEANT carries a newspaper.*

FORD: (*Surprised*) Hello, Bob!

BRODERICK: I hope I'm not interrupting your breakfast?

FORD: No, we've just finished. Would you like a cup of
             tea?

BRODERICK: No, thank you. (*Holding up the newspaper*) Well
             – have you seen this?

FORD: What is it?

BRODERICK: It's The London Dispatch.

FORD: No, we don't get it.

BRODERICK: (*Handing FORD the paper*) Well, take a look at
             it. There's an article by young Craven.

FORD: (*Taking the paper*) What – in the Dispatch?

BRODERICK: (*Significantly*) Yes. Read it.

*FORD opens the newspaper and sees the article is illustrated
with a photograph of the houseboat High Tor. The headline title
of the article is: "Murder of a Frogman" by Robin Craven.
FORD is puzzled and looks up at BRODERICK.*

FORD: What the devil does this mean?

BRODERICK: (*Seriously*) Read it, Mike.

*FORD looks at BRODERICK then turns and reads the
newspaper.*

BRODERICK: (*To ROGER; making conversation whilst FORD
             reads*) Well, Roger – how's life?

ROGER: Oh, fine. Are you any good at geography,
             Sergeant?

BRODERICK: (*Very confidently*) Yes, sure. What's the
             problem?

ROGER: What does parallel longitudinal mean?

70

BRODERICK: (*Stunned*) Parallel – what?

ROGER: Longitudinal.

BRODERICK: (*Playing for time*) Oh, longitudinal!

ROGER: (*Watching BRODERICK*) Yes.

BRODERICK: Well, now – er …

FORD: (*Looking up; to ROGER*) Have you finished your breakfast, Roger?

ROGER: Yes, Dad.

FORD: Well, run along – there's a good chap. (*As ROGER hesitates; seriously*) Go on, Roger!

ROGER: (*A shade reluctant*) Oh – all right.

ROGER smiles at BRODERICK and goes out.

FORD: (*To BRODERICK; holding up the newspaper*) What the hell does this mean?

BRODERICK: It means Craven knows a great deal more about Rocello than we do.

FORD: (*Annoyed; in fact definitely angry*) Yes, but where did he get this information from?

BRODERICK: I don't know.

FORD: Do you think it's true?

BRODERICK: Well, it reads pretty authentic. (*Takes the newspaper from FORD and looks at it*) You see what it says. "Count Paragi confirmed that Rocello was a Frogman and a member of the 12th Flotilla."

FORD: Yes, but what put young Craven onto this Count Paragi in the first place?

BRODERICK: I don't know.

The doorbell rings.

FORD: (*Angry; pointing to the newspaper*) Either this is a lot of nonsense or Craven's onto something – in which case he'd no business to write that article, he should have come straight to us.

The doorbell continues.

71

BRODERICK: (*Smiling*) He's a journalist, Mike. It's his job to write articles.

FORD: (*Still angry*) Bob, this isn't petty larceny, it's a murder case! The moment young Craven discovered Rocello's identity he should have ...

The doorbell rings again.

FORD: Roger, for goodness sake answer the door!

BRODERICK: (*Trying to pacify FORD*) Mike, you know Craven. For years he's been trying to get his nose into Fleet Street. This was probably a lucky break so far as he was concerned.

FORD: Well, it's not a lucky break so far as I'm concerned! What do you think the Superintendent's going to say when he sees that article and then reads my report saying we know nothing about Rocello – we don't even know who he is.

ROGER enters.

FORD: (*Turning*) Yes – what is it, Roger?

ROGER: There's a Mr Craven at the door, Father. He wants a word with you.

FORD looks at BRODERICK.

BRODERICK: (*Nodding*) I phoned him as soon as I saw the paper. I said you'd probably want to see him.

FORD: You bet I want to see him! (*To ROGER*) Show the gentleman in, Roger!

ROGER goes out.

BRODERICK: Look, Mike, don't think I'm trying to give you advice – but if I were you I wouldn't let Craven think he's discovered anything we don't already know. (*Smiling*) You can still blow your top off, if you feel like it.

ROBIN CRAVEN comes into the kitchen.

CRAVEN: Good morning, Inspector!

72

FORD: Hello, Craven.

CRAVEN: I understand you want to see me?

FORD: Yes, I do. (*Introducing BRODERICK*) Oh, this is Sergeant Broderick – he spoke to you on the telephone.

CRAVEN: Good morning, Sergeant.

BRODERICK nods.

FORD: (*Picking up the newspaper*) I've just read your article. Where did you get this information from?

CRAVEN: What information, Inspector?

FORD: (*Trying to intimidate CRAVEN*) You know what I mean – this stuff about Rocello.

CRAVEN: You mean, about his being a friend of Count Paragi's?

FORD: I mean the whole story! How did you know he was a friend of Paragi's? How did you know he was a Frogman during the war? How did you know …

CRAVEN: (*Stopping FORD; calmly*) Now wait a minute! One at a time, please! (*Smiling at BRODERICK*) Is he always like this?

BRODERICK: The Inspector's annoyed. He feels you should have consulted us before you wrote the article.

CRAVEN: Oh, does he? That's interesting. (*To FORD; peering at him*) Why should I have consulted you?

FORD: (*Indicating the newspaper*) This article contains information which ought never to have been made public.

CRAVEN: That's an unusual point of view, Inspector, if I may say so.

FORD: (*Angrily*) It doesn't matter whether it's an unusual point of view or not, the point is …

BRODERICK: (*Quietly; to CRAVEN*) How did you find out about Rocello?

CRAVEN hesitates, then takes the note out of his inside pocket.

CRAVEN: Someone sent me this note.

FORD takes the note from CRAVEN and looks at it. He sees the drawing of the Frogman with the words, written underneath the drawing: Portrait of R. 1943. FORD looks up.

FORD: When did you get this?

CRAVEN: Last Tuesday morning.

FORD passes the note to BRODERICK.

FORD: Who sent it?

CRAVEN: I don't know. It was dropped through my letterbox.

FORD: Was there an envelope?

CRAVEN: No.

BRODERICK: (*Looking up from the note*) What made you think this had anything to do with Rocello?

CRAVEN: The letter R. and the fact that – well, the fact that I couldn't think of anyone else. Besides, I'd been making inquiries about Rocello, trying to find out a few things about him. When I got that note I decided to try the Italian library at the British Museum. (*To FORD: smiling*) I thoroughly recommend the British Museum, Inspector.

FORD: (*Taking the note from BRODERICK*) What else did you find out?

CRAVEN: What do you want?

FORD: Did you find out anything else – other than what's in the Dispatch?

CRAVEN: No, it's all in the article, Inspector.

FORD: You say you contacted Count Paragi?

CRAVEN: Yes, I did. I sent him a cable; he replied by return.

FORD: Saying what?

74

CRAVEN: (*Pointing to the newspaper*) Saying that he knew Rocello during the war and that they were both members of the 12ᵗʰ Flotilla. That was the midget submarine crowd – the first of the Frogmen. (*A sudden thought*) I say, that's a good title, isn't it? The First of the Frogmen. I must bear that in mind.

FORD: Yes, and there's something else you must bear in mind, Craven.

CRAVEN: (*Interested*) Oh – what's that?

FORD: If you get another note like this, if anyone contacts you about Rocello, come straight to us. Never mind the newspapers!

CRAVEN: But I'm a journalist, Inspector – that's how I earn a living.

BRODERICK: You know what the Inspector means.

FORD: I don't want to be difficult about this, Craven, and I'm not trying to set myself up as an unofficial censor, but if you get information which might be of value then it's your duty to pass it on to us, not just slap it down on paper.

CRAVEN: (*Grinning; indicating the newspaper again*) Didn't you know about Rocello then – didn't you know who he was?

FORD: Of course we knew who he was, that's not the point. (*Looks at the note he is holding*) I'll take care of this, Craven.

CRAVEN: (*Hesitantly*) Is that necessary?

FORD: Yes, I'm afraid it is. (*Nodding*) All right, Craven. I'll see you out.

FORD puts the note down on the table.

CRAVEN: (*To BRODERICK, as he goes out*) Au revoir, Sergeant.

BRODERICK: Goodbye, Craven.

FORD goes out with CRAVEN. BRODERICK stands by the table. He picks up the note and studies it; turns it over, examines the paper; holds it up to the light to look at the watermark. FORD returns; he is carrying one of ROGER's exercise books.

FORD: (*To BRODERICK; quietly*) Let me have a look at that note, Bob.

BRODERICK: (*Indicating the exercise book*) What's that you've got?

FORD: It's one of Roger's exercise books.

BRODERICK: (*Puzzled*) What do you want that for?

FORD doesn't reply; he opens the exercise book and takes the note from BRODERICK. The page shows part of an English essay with several spelling corrections and a final comment in HENDERSON's handwriting. The comment reads: "You can do better than this".

FORD puts down the exercise book and picks up the book which ROGER was reading at the breakfast table. He turns to the flyleaf on which is scribbled in pencil, in HENDERSON's handwriting, the word "Suavitor in modo, fortiter in re".

BRODERICK: That's Henderson's handwriting!

FORD: Yes!

BRODERICK: But why should Henderson send a note to Robin Craven?

FORD: Presumably because he wanted him to know about Rocello.

BRODERICK: But why? He must have known that Craven would write an article about it.

FORD: (*Quietly; bewildered*) I don't get it. I just don't get it. If this is Henderson's handwriting then obviously he knows all about the Italian. In which case …

BRODERICK: In which case, why didn't he tell you about Rocello when you interviewed him?

76

FORD: He told me he didn't know Rocello; he said
                   he knew nothing about him.

BRODERICK picks up the exercise book and looks at it.

BRODERICK: Well, he must have known something or he
                   couldn't have written the note. (*Looks up at
                   FORD*) Mike, if I were you I'd have another
                   word with Henderson. Be perfectly frank with
                   him. Tell him about Craven; tell him about
                   the note; tell him everything we know – and
                   see what happens.

CUT TO: DAVID HENDERSON's Study.

*HENDERSON is sitting in an armchair, slowly filling his pipe
from a tobacco pouch. He is talking to FORD who is sitting on
the settee facing him. The INSPECTOR looks serious and
distinctly worried. HENDERSON appears calm, unperturbed.*

HENDERSON: Well, I may be a little dense, Inspector, but I
                   don't see what you're getting at. You say
                   that's my handwriting and I say that it isn't.
                   Obviously therefore, it's my word against
                   yours.

FORD: It isn't quite as simple as that, Mr Henderson.

HENDERSON: Indeed?

FORD: No, sir. when I suspected that you might have
                   written the note, I sent it, together with a
                   sample of your handwriting, to Mr Stacey
                   Boyd. Mr Stacey Boyd confirmed my
                   suspicions.

HENDERSON: And who, may I ask, is Mr Stacey Boyd?

FORD: He's a handwriting expert, sir. He's been a
                   recognised authority for a considerable
                   number of years.

HENDERSON: (*With the suggestion of a smile*) Perhaps it's
                   about time he retired, Inspector.

FORD: I'm afraid I don't find that amusing, Mr Henderson – so far as I'm concerned it's a very serious matter.

HENDERSON: You say you sent Mr Stacey Boyd a sample of my handwriting?

FORD: Yes; I found an exercise book of Roger's and a book you lent him for the holidays. (*Looks at HENDERSON*) The one on the Italian lakes.

HENDERSON: Oh, yes.

FORD: You'd written something on the flyleaf, Mr Henderson.

HENDERSON: Had I? Oh yes, I remember now. That was the quotation. Suavitor in modo, fortiter in re …

FORD: That's right. I asked you what it meant – you may remember?

HENDERSON: Yes, I remember. But do you remember, Inspector – that's the point? (*Smiling*) Suavitor in modo, fortiter in re …

FORD: (*Watching HENDERSON*) Gentle in the manner but vigorous in the deed.

HENDERSON: (*Nodding*) Excellent, Inspector! Full marks!

FORD: (*Leaning forward*) Mr Henderson, doesn't it strike you as being a rather odd coincidence that that quotation should be inscribed on the back of the dead man's watch, as well as on the flyleaf of your book?

HENDERSON: It does indeed.

FORD: Well, can't you offer me an explanation, sir?

HENDERSON: No, I'm afraid I can't. And even if I could I doubt whether you'd believe it.

FORD: What made you write the quotation down in the first place?

HENDERSON: I didn't want to forget it.

FORD:	You mean, you read it somewhere and just jotted it down?
HENDERSON:	Exactly.
FORD:	Well, where did you read it, sir – in a book?
HENDERSON:	(*Smiling*) Where else could I have read it, Inspector?
FORD:	(*Looking at HENDERSON; quietly*) It's a quotation. You might have seen it on a gravestone, sir.
HENDERSON:	On a gravestone?
FORD:	Yes. It's just the kind of thing some people would put on a gravestone.

HENDERSON looks at FORD with a faint suggestion of surprise, then he gives a little smile and rises.

HENDERSON:	It is indeed. We might bear it in mind, Inspector. (*Looking at his watch*) Now if you'll excuse me.

FORD rises.

FORD:	You're not going away at all, are you, sir?
HENDERSON:	Away?
FORD:	During the holidays?
HENDERSON:	No, I shall be here the whole time, Inspector – in case you want me.

FORD looks at HENDERSON and nods his approval.

CUT TO: The Tow Path leading up to the houseboat Shangri La.

CHRIS REYNOLDS appears on the path carrying a suitcase. He is in his late twenties and his clothes and manner are a cross between a Teddy Boy and a West End hawker. He arrives at the houseboat and goes on board.

CUT TO: The Interior of the main cabin of the Shangri La.

CHRIS enters, puts down his suitcase, and mops his brow with a handkerchief.

CHRIS: (*Calling*) Billie!

CHRIS looks round the cabin; takes stock of his surroundings.

CHRIS: (*Calling*) Billie, it's Chris!

CHRIS crosses to the door on the left and opens it and pops his head into the adjoining cabin.

CHRIS: (*Calling*) Billie, where are you?

CHRIS goes into the cabin and then returns a moment later scratching his head and looking very puzzled. He returns to the main door, opens it and looks up towards the door.

CHRIS: (Calling; louder) Billie, it's Chris! Where the 'ell are you?!

CHRIS returns to the centre of the cabin; looks about him, then kneels down and flicks open his suitcase. Suddenly something catches his eyes and he rises and moves in front of the centre table. He stoops down, puts his hand under the table, and picks up the object which has attracted his attention. It is one of HENDERSON's chessmen – a Bishop. CHRIS looks down at the chessman, obviously puzzled.

CUT TO: The Living Room of MICHAEL FORD's House. Evening.

FORD is standing by the table lighting a cigarette. His jacket is over the back of a chair; his sleeves rolled up. He looks a shade worried. DR SHELDON comes out of the bedroom carrying his medical bag.

SHELDON: (*Smiling*) Well, I shouldn't lose any sleep over that young man.

FORD: (*Anxiously*) What is it, doctor?

SHELDON: Well, whatever it is he'll be as right as rain tomorrow morning, I'm sure of that.

FORD: (*Puzzled*) But he was perfectly all right an hour ago and then suddenly he was complaining of a headache and pains and feeling violently sick.

SHELDON: (*Nodding*) I've given him some bicarbonate of soda, he'll be all right in the morning.

FORD: But what is it? Are you sure it's not serious?

SHELDON picks up his hat and gloves from the settee.

SHELDON: I'm quite sure. He went to the pictures this afternoon, didn't he?

FORD: Why, yes. (*Faintly alarmed*) Do you think he caught something?

SHELDON: (*Laughing*) No, but I think he bought something – in fact I know he did. Four choc ices and an orangeade.

FORD: Oh, my God!

SHELDON: (*A warning*) Now don't you let on I told you!

FORD starts to laugh; both amused and relieved.

FORD: The little devil! I asked him if he'd had anything to eat.

SHELDON: (*Amused*) Give me a ring tomorrow morning if you're not happy about him – but he'll be all right, I'm sure. (*Turning towards the door*) Have you seen Henderson recently?

FORD: (*A shade surprised by the question*) Yes; I saw him the day before yesterday.

SHELDON: He called round to see me the other day, said he'd been having trouble with his shoulder. Somehow – I don't think he had.

FORD: What do you mean?

SHELDON: I may be wrong but I think he wanted to take a look at Katherine.

FORD: Why should he want to do that?

SHELDON: I don't know, it was just a feeling I had. (*Looking at FORD*) He knew that someone had reported

81

	him to the police but apparently he didn't know who it was.
FORD:	He knew who it was all right, I told him.
SHELDON:	(*Surprised*) Oh, did you?
FORD:	(*Nodding*) I thought it best to be perfectly frank. Did he meet Miss Walters?
SHELDON:	Yes.
FORD:	Did he say anything?
SHELDON:	He said that someone had told you that they'd seen him near the houseboat; he gave us to understand that he didn't know who it was and that the whole idea was ridiculous.
FORD:	What did Miss Walters say?
SHELDON:	She didn't say anything; I'm afraid we were both a little embarrassed.
FORD:	What happened after he left – did Miss Walters make any comment?
SHELDON:	No; except that she's still convinced that it was Henderson she saw.
FORD:	(*Quietly; nodding*) It was Henderson all right. I don't think there's any doubt about that. What was he like with Miss Walters? I mean, was he pleasant or …
SHELDON:	Oh, very pleasant. Curiously enough Katherine rather liked him.

FORD nods.

FORD: That doesn't surprise me.

FORD and SHELDON pass into the entrance hall as the doorbell starts ringing.

CUT TO: The Entrance Hall of MICHAEL FORD's House.
FORD and SHELDON enter from the lounge. FORD crosses and puts his hand on the front door latch.

SHELDON: If I'm passing I'll drop in tomorrow morning, but Roger will be all right – I'm sure.
FORD: Thank you, doctor.

FORD opens the door. CHRIS REYNOLDS is standing in the doorway; he is wearing narrow grey trousers and an extremely long jacket.

CHRIS: Inspector Ford?
FORD: (*Surprised*) Yes?
CHRIS: If you're not too busy, chum – I'd like a word with you.

SHELDON looks at FORD and gives a little smile.

FORD: Who are you exactly? Who sent you here?
CHRIS: No one sent me. I called at the police station – they said you was off duty, so I looked you up in the phone book. Can I come in?
FORD: Yes, all right, Mr –?
CHRIS: (*Pushing past FORD*) Reynolds. Chris Reynolds.

CUT TO: MICHAEL FORD's Living Room.

CHRIS enters; slowly he takes stock of his surroundings, then turns towards the alcove as Ford re-enters the living room.

FORD: Now, Mr Reynolds – what can I do for you?
CHRIS: They tell me you're the big cheese around here, is that right?
FORD: I'm afraid I don't know what you mean?
CHRIS: (*Pleasantly*) You know what I mean. The big noise. The big white chief.
FORD: (*Facing CHRIS; bluntly*) What is it you want?
CHRIS: Do you know my sister?
FORD: (*Puzzled*) Your sister?
CHRIS: Yes. Billie. Billie Reynolds. She's got a houseboat down here – the Shangri La.
FORD: Oh! Oh, yes – I know your sister.
CHRIS: Well, she's disappeared.

FORD: Disappeared?

CHRIS: That's right – disappeared. Vamoosed.

FORD: Suppose you start at the beginning, Mr Reynolds, and tell me what this is all about?

CHRIS: Well, I don't know what it's all about, chum – if I did I wouldn't be here. All I know is Billie's disappeared an' I don't like it. I don't like it, chum.

FORD: When did Miss Reynolds disappear?

CHRIS: I don't know. I got here on Monday afternoon expecting her to greet me with open arms and – (*A shrug*) nothin' doing.

FORD: Was she expecting you?

CHRIS: 'Course she was expecting me! I brought her four dozen nylons. (*A gesture*) All paid for, chum – every single one of 'em.

FORD: Have you been down here before, Reynolds?

CHRIS: No, never – an' never again. It's a dead an' alive hole so far as I'm concerned. Soon as I know Billie's all right, I'm off.

FORD: (*Watching CHRIS*) What makes you think she's not all right?

CHRIS: I've told you – she's disappeared! Blimey, I've been waiting for her to show up since Monday afternoon.

FORD: Perhaps you misunderstood your sister; perhaps she's in London somewhere waiting for you?

CHRIS: (*Shaking his head*) There's been no misunderstanding, chum, Billie phoned me a fortnight ago and told me to be at the houseboat on the fourteenth, that was last Monday.

FORD: Did she say anything else?

CHRIS: No, except that she wanted the nylons. Four dozen of 'em. Blimey, she doesn't 'alf use some nylons our Billie. I reckon she eats 'em, I do honest.

FORD: Are you staying on the houseboat?

CHRIS: Yes, I've told you, I've been there since Monday afternoon waiting for Billie to show up – an' proper browned off I am too! My Gawd, who'd want to live on a houseboat! You can't hear a ruddy thing except the water. Lap – lap – lap – it fair drives you up the wall.

FORD: Your sister seems to like it, she's been down here nearly three years now.

CHRIS: Yes, I know. I don't know what she sees in it – unless she's got a boyfriend down here. (*Looking at FORD*) Has she got a boyfriend?

FORD: You'd better ask your sister that question.

CHRIS: I'd like to ask her – but where the 'ell is she?

FORD: You say you arrived here on Monday afternoon?

CHRIS: That's right, half past four. I told Billie I'd be here by 'alf past four. On the dot, I was. Never been late for an appointment yet.

FORD: Have you made any inquiries about your sister?

CHRIS: Sure – but nobody's seen her. I just don't understand it. (*Shaking his head*) This isn't like Billie. Once before when we arranged to meet she 'ad to call it off but she sent me a flippin telegram. That's what beats me, why didn't she send me a flippin telegram this time?

FORD: (*Quietly*) All right, Reynolds, I'll make inquiries. Where can I get in touch with you?

CHRIS: Shangri La. (*He looks up to the sky*)

FORD: (*Casually*) Why did you ask me if your sister had a boyfriend?

CHRIS: Well, I thought if she 'ad he might be able to help us.

FORD: Had you got anyone in mind?

CHRIS: No, course I 'adn't got anyone in mind. But there must be somebody down here otherwise Billie'd never stick it, I'm sure of that.

FORD: Did she ever mention anyone to you?

CHRIS: No, never, but –

FORD: (*Quite friendly*) Go on …

CHRIS absent mindedly takes the chessman out of his pocket and twists it between his fingers.

CHRIS: Well, about a year ago I was in a bit of a fix. I needed fifty quid. I was pretty desperate I can assure you. In the end Billie stumped up all right. (*A shrug*) Knowing Billie she must have touched somebody.

FORD: But you've no idea who it was?

CHRIS: (*Shaking his head*) Nope.

FORD: When did you last see Billie?

CHRIS: About four months ago – the end of April I think it was. She came up to Town for a weekend.

FORD: (*Dismissing CHRIS*) All right, Reynolds. I'll make inquiries and if there's any news I'll get in touch with you.

CHRIS: Okay.

CHRIS is about to replace the chessman in his pocket; he suddenly looks at it.

CHRIS: I found this in the cabin. Don't know what the 'ell it was doing there.

FORD slowly takes the Bishop from CHRIS and looks at it.

FORD: (*After a moment*) You say you found it on the houseboat?

CHRIS: That's right, in the cabin, under the flippin table.

FORD: Could your sister play chess?

CHRIS: (*Laughing*) Billie? What d'you think, chum?

FORD: May I keep this?

CHRIS: (*Looking at FORD*) Sure – if you want to. If you get any news let me know.

FORD: (*Still looking at the Bishop*) Yes, I will.

CHRIS goes out through the alcove. FORD looks up and then suddenly follows him. We hear the front door open and close and then FORD returns to the living room. He is still examining the chessman. After a moment he puts it down on the table, crosses to the sideboard, and picks up the local telephone directory. He flicks the pages, finds the number he wants and crosses to the telephone and dials a number.

FORD: (*On the telephone*) Medlow 843, please … Thank you … Hello? … Mr Merson? … This is Inspector Ford. I'm sorry to trouble you, sir – but when you called round the other morning you mentioned a friend of yours … No … No, a lady friend … Yes, that's right … Well, I want some information about her and I think you may be able to help me … Yes, certainly – tonight would suit me better as a matter of fact … All right, Mr Merson, I'll expect you about half past eight … Thank you, sir.

FORD replaces the receiver and picks up the Bishop.

CUT TO: MICHAEL FORD's Lounge.

RALPH MERSON is sitting in an armchair. FORD is standing facing him.

MERSON: (*Looking at the Bishop*) I've never seen it before.

FORD: Are you sure?

MERSON: Of course I'm sure!

FORD: Do you play chess, Mr Merson?

MERSON: Well, I can play – but I haven't played for years.

FORD: Did you ever play chess with Miss Reynolds?

MERSON: (*Astonished*) Are you serious?

FORD smiles and takes the Bishop out of MERSON's hand and puts it down on the table. MERSON rises.

MERSON: Look, what's the point of all these questions? (*Pointing to the Bishop*) What's this got to do with Billie Reynolds?

FORD: It was found in her cabin.

MERSON: (*A shrug*) I still don't see why you should ask … (*He stops; looks at FORD, obviously alarmed*) Has something happened to Billie?

FORD: (*Quietly; nodding*) She's disappeared.

MERSON: (*Astonished*) Disappeared?

FORD: Yes.

MERSON: (*With a little laugh*) Who told you that?

FORD: Her brother told me. He was here about an hour ago. Apparently he came down from London expecting to stay a few days with his sister. She wasn't here when he arrived and he hasn't seen her since.

MERSON: I didn't know Billie had a brother.

FORD: I can assure you she has, and if I were you I'd give the gentleman a very wide berth.

MERSON: I've every intention of giving him a wide berth. (*Irritated*) I'm not interested in Billie's brother.

FORD: No; but he's interested in you.

MERSON: What do you mean?

FORD: He asked me if his sister had a boyfriend.

MERSON: (*Quietly; alarmed*) Good God, you didn't tell him …

FORD: I didn't tell him anything. (*Pointing a finger at MERSON; with authority*) But I'm telling you, Merson, if Reynolds tries to contact you, have nothing to do with him. Unless I'm mistaken he's a pretty tough baby.

MERSON: (*A shade apprehensive*) Why did he ask if she had a boyfriend?

FORD: Isn't it obvious why? Billie's disappeared, he probably thought she was staying with him.

88

MERSON: (*Shaking his head*) I haven't seen Billie for over a week. A week last Friday I think it was.

FORD: And you've no idea where she is?

MERSON: Not the slightest.

FORD: Had she any other 'boyfriend', besides yourself?

MERSON: (*Resenting the tone*) Really, Inspector – I wouldn't know!

FORD: Merson, tell me, did you ever lend Billie fifty pounds?

MERSON: No, of course not! Why do you ask?

FORD: Did she ever try to borrow fifty pounds from you?

MERSON: (*Hesitant*) Yes – about a year ago. (*Shaking his head*) I wasn't wearing it.

FORD: Who did she borrow the money from?

MERSON: I don't know. I don't even know whether she did borrow it from anyone.

FORD: (*Quietly*) She borrowed it. (*Dismissing MERSON*) All right, Merson. I'll let you know if anything develops. And if Billie gets in touch with you phone me immediately.

MERSON: (*Nodding*) Yes, all right. (*He hesitates*) Inspector, you don't think there's anything to worry about …

FORD: Worry about?

MERSON: Yes. You don't think anything's happened to Billie?

FORD: (*Watching him*) What could have happened to her?

MERSON: I don't know. I – I was just thinking, that's all.

MERSON looks at FORD, hesitates then goes out through the alcove followed by the INSPECTOR. After a moment ROGER emerges from the bedroom; he is wearing a dressing gown over his pyjamas and bedroom slippers. FORD returns.

FORD: (*To ROGER; surprised*) Hello! What are you doing?

ROGER: I'm thirsty, Dad. Can I have a drink?

FORD: Yes, all right. I'll get you a glass of water – get back into bed.

| ROGER: | (*Seriously*) I'd sooner have an orangeade, Dad. I still feel a bit sick and water always … |
| FORD: | You wouldn't like a couple of choc ices? |

ROGER looks at his father, a shade undecided how to take this; suddenly he grins.

FORD:	(*Smiling*) How do you feel now?
ROGER:	Much better.
FORD:	All right, get back into bed.

ROGER turns, notices the chessman on the table.

| ROGER: | (*Surprised*) Has Mr Henderson been here? |
| FORD: | Mr Henderson? No, of course he hasn't. Why do you ask? |

ROGER points to the Bishop on the table.

ROGER:	That's one of his chessmen.
FORD:	(*Picking up the Bishop*) This is?
ROGER:	Yes.
FORD:	Are you sure?
ROGER:	(*Laughing*) Of course I'm sure! I've played with it often enough. If you look carefully there's a scratch on it, right down the left hand side.

FORD picks up the Bishop and examines it.

| FORD: | (*After a moment*) Yes, so there is, Roger. (*Quietly*) So there is … |

FORD looks serious and very worried.

CUT TO: DAVID HENDERSON's Study. The next morning.
MRS WILLIAMS shows FORD into the room.

MRS WILLIAMS:	Mr Henderson shouldn't be very long, sir. He's just gone up to the main building.
FORD:	Yes, all right, Mrs Williams. I'll wait.
MRS WILLIAMS:	Can I get you anything, sir?

FORD:	No, thank you. (*Apparently an afterthought*) Oh, Mrs Williams – do you know a person – a girl – called Billie Reynolds?
MRS WILLIAMS:	I do! I do indeed. A brazen hussy. She called to see Mr Henderson about ten days ago.
FORD:	(*Pleasantly*) Did she? What did she want to see him about – do you know?
MRS WILLIAMS:	(*On guard*) I'm afraid, I don't know sir – you'll have to ask Mr Henderson that.

HENDERSON enters carrying a pile of envelopes and several books.

HENDERSON:	(*Pleasantly, but surprised*) Hello, Inspector! (*Hands Mrs Williams the envelopes*) Get these off to the post sometime today, Mrs Williams.
MRS WILLIAMS:	Yes, certainly, sir.

MRS WILLIAMS takes the envelopes from HENDERSON and goes out.

HENDERSON:	(*To FORD*) I've been doing reports all morning. It's a job I detest. The Head's so pernickety about it too, he simply won't let up.
FORD:	(*Seriously*) Mr Henderson, do you know a girl called Billie Reynolds?
HENDERSON:	Billie Reynolds? Yes, I do. She's got a houseboat down here.
FORD:	That's right, sir.
HENDERSON:	(*Laughing*) She's quite a character. We had a spot of trouble with her about twelve months ago. The boys used to bathe in the river and she insisted on joining them.

FORD:	(*Watching HENDERSON*) When did you last see Miss Reynolds?
HENDERSON:	(*Surprised*) Me?
FORD:	Yes.
HENDERSON:	Well, as a matter of fact I saw her about ten days ago.
FORD:	Where?
HENDERSON:	Here – she called round to see me. (*Smiling; anticipating FORD's question*) Why did she call round to see me? Well, since last year the Head's forbidden the boys to go anywhere near the river. Billie said she felt guilty about it and she promised to behave herself if we lifted the ban.
FORD:	Was that the only reason she called to see you?
HENDERSON:	Yes, of course. But why all these questions about Billie Reynolds?
FORD:	She's disappeared, sir.
HENDERSON:	Well, you won't find her here, Inspector.
FORD:	Did you ever visit Miss Reynolds, sir?
HENDERSON:	You mean – at the houseboat?
FORD:	Yes.
HENDERSON:	(*Nodding*) Once – a year ago when all the flapdoodle was on. The Head sent me down to have a talk to her. (*Laughing*) I didn't get very far I'm afraid.
FORD:	You haven't been there recently?
HENDERSON:	What, to the houseboat?
FORD nods.	
HENDERSON:	Good heavens, no! We weren't exactly on visiting terms, Inspector.

FORD looks at HENDERSON for a moment; HENDERSON meets his gaze.

FORD: Do you play chess, Mr Henderson?

HENDERSON: (*A moment*) Yes, I do.

FORD: Have you a chess set?

HENDERSON: Why, yes, of course.

FORD: May I see it?

HENDERSON looks at FORD; faintly amused.

HENDERSON: What is all this?

FORD: (*Seriously*) May I see it, sir?

HENDERSON hesitates then turns towards the writing desk. He opens the desk and takes out the wooden chess box and board. He puts them down on the table that is facing the chair FORD is sitting on.

HENDERSON: There we are, Inspector. I also have a pack of cards, a backgammon board, a set of dominoes, and a very old Put-and-Take, - would you care to see them?

FORD opens the box, takes out the chessmen, and begins to arrange them on the board. HENDERSON watches FORD as he does this. Finally, the set is complete except for one Bishop.

FORD: (*Slowly; looking up*) There appears to be a Bishop missing, Mr Henderson.

HENDERSON stares down at the board; apparently puzzled.

HENDERSON: Yes, so there does. It must be in the desk. (*He turns towards the desk*)

FORD: (*Shaking his head; stopping HENDERSON*) It's not in the desk, sir.

HENDERSON: (*Turning*) No?

FORD: No. (*He takes the Bishop out of his pocket and holds it up*) It's here, Mr Henderson. It was found in Billie Reynolds's cabin.

HENDERSON crosses and takes the Bishop out of FORD's hand. He looks at it for a moment.

HENDERSON: (*Calmly; returning the Bishop to FORD*) I
               don't think that's mine, Inspector – although
               it certainly looks like it.

*HENDERSON crosses to the desk, rearranges the contents, and
then searches one of the cubby holes. After a moment he turns
and holds up a chessman – it is a Bishop.*

HENDERSON: Ah, here it is! It must have fallen out of the
               box.

*HENDERSON moves across to INSPECTOR and puts the Bishop
in its correct place on the chessboard. He smiles at FORD.*

CUT TO: INSPECTOR FORD's Office.

*FORD is sitting behind his desk. SERGEANT BRODERICK is
sitting in a chair opposite the desk. He is holding the chessman.*

BRODERICK: He could have replaced it, I suppose – but
               how the devil are we going to prove it? (*He
               looks at the Bishop*) There must be hundreds
               of shops that sell chessmen like this.

FORD: In which case he might be telling the truth,
               perhaps that doesn't belong to him.

BRODERICK: Then Roger's mistaken?

FORD: Well, the boy could be mistaken, he's not
               infallible.

BRODERICK: (*Shaking his head*) I don't think he was
               mistaken, Mike – and neither do you.
               (*Pointing to the Bishop*) He told you about the
               scratch and here it is. This is Henderson's all
               right.

FORD: The thing that beats me is that Henderson
               doesn't seem to be rattled by all this, he was
               as cool as a cucumber when I saw him
               yesterday afternoon.

BRODERICK: He's not rattled because at the moment he's
                very sure of himself; but you wait – he'll get
                rattled towards the end.

FORD: I wish to goodness I knew what this was all
                about? Why should a man like Henderson get
                mixed up with a woman like Billie Reynolds?

BRODERICK: My dear Mike, if we knew the answer to that
                one …

PC SANDERS enters; he is a uniformed policeman.

BRODERICK: Yes, Sanders?

SANDERS: There's a Mr Merson to see the Inspector, he
                says it's urgent.

BRODERICK looks at FORD who immediately nods his head.

BRODERICK: All right – show him in.

SANDERS goes out and FORD rises from his desk.

FORD: Merson? I wonder if Reynolds has been onto
                him?

BRODERICK: I wouldn't be surprised.

SANDERS returns with RALPH MERSON.

MERSON: (*To FORD; obviously very worried*) I'm sorry
                to trouble you, Inspector, but I thought
                perhaps … (*He hesitates; looks at
                BRODERICK*)

FORD: This is Sergeant Broderick – you've met
                before.

MERSON: Oh, yes, of course.

FORD: Well, what is it, Mr Merson? What can I do
                for you?

*MERSON takes a girl's earring out of his pocket; it is a large
costume jewellery style earring.*

MERSON: (*Obviously agitated*) I received this this
                morning, through the post.

BRODERICK: (*Looking at MERSON's hand*) What is it?

MERSON: It's one of Billie's earrings.

FORD:	(*Taking the earring from MERSON*) Are you sure?
MERSON:	Of course I'm sure! I gave them to her just over a year ago.
FORD:	(*Examining the earring*) You say it came through the post?
MERSON:	(*Taking a piece of paper out of his pocket and an envelope*) Yes. There was a note with it – here it is.

FORD takes the note and looks at it.

FORD:	(*Reading the note*) "If you'd like the other one try Fallow End" …
MERSON:	What does it mean – "if you'd like the other one"?
FORD:	Well, presumably it means – if you'd like the other earring.
MERSON:	Oh. Oh, I see.
FORD:	(*Watching MERSON; curious*) Does that make sense to you?
MERSON:	(*Hesitantly*) Well – in a way, yes. You see, whenever Billie and I had a quarrel she always threatened to give the earrings back to me …
BRODERICK:	Threatened to give them back to you?
MERSON:	Well – you know what women are when they lose their temper.
FORD:	Have you had a quarrel then, – recently?
MERSON:	No. No, certainly not. I told you, I haven't seen Billie for days.
FORD:	(*Looking at the note*) Do you think Miss Reynolds wrote this?
MERSON:	No. No, I'm sure she didn't.
FORD:	Is that the envelope?

MERSON nods and gives FORD the envelope he is holding.

MERSON: (*Pointing to the postmark*) It was posted in London by the look of things.

FORD: (*Quietly; looking at the envelope*) Yes.

BRODERICK picks up the note and is about to look at it when MERSON turns towards him.

MERSON: (*To BRODERICK*) Where is Fallow End, the name sounds vaguely familiar?

BRODERICK: It's a small creek about fifty yards from Cane Lock. The river bends at a place called Fallow. It used to be a bit of a dead end but they widened it out a couple of years ago.

MERSON: It's quite a way from the houseboats.

BRODERICK: Oh, yes. I should say half a mile.

BRODERICK looks at the note, then quickly glances across at FORD who catches his eye and gives a little nod.

FORD: (*Rising from the desk*) All right, Mr Merson. Thank you very much.

MERSON: (*Hesitantly; looking first at BRODERICK then across at FORD*) You don't think anything has happened to Billie and the person who … (*He stops*)

FORD: And the person who what?

MERSON: And the person who wrote that note thought that … (*Apparently lost for words*) I don't quite know what I was going to say.

FORD looks at MERSON for a moment and then nods to BRODERICK.

FORD: Show Mr Merson out, Sergeant.

MERSON and BRODERICK go out. FORD crosses in front of the desk and leans against it deep in thought. BRODERICK returns.

BRODERICK: (*To FORD; a shade excited*) Mike, that's Henderson's handwriting – there's no doubt about it! It's the same handwriting as before.

FORD: (*Turning; quietly*) Yes, I know.

BRODERICK: (*Looking down at the note*) Why in God's name should Henderson send …

FORD: (*Quietly; interrupting BRODERICK*) Bob, listen. I want a search party. I want every available man on the station. I want the river combed – dragged if necessary – right from Billie's houseboat down to Fallow End.

BRODERICK: (*A shade surprised*) All right, Mike. (*Smiling*) But I think you're on a wild goose chase.

FORD: Why? What do you think?

BRODERICK: I think Billie's given our friend Merson the brush-off. It's my bet she's in London somewhere – probably at a swank hotel with a middle-aged sugar daddy.

FORD: I hope you're right, but I don't think you are. I think she's dead and we'll find the body in the river.

BRODERICK: I'll bet you ten bob we don't.

FORD glances down at the note again, then looks up.

FORD: (*Nodding; quietly*) All right, Sergeant. Ten bob.

CUT TO: A Stretch of the river near Medlow.

Numerous cars are parked on the banks of the river and a great many people – uniformed and plain clothes police – are parading the towpath. Several of the plain clothes police are in rowing boats on the river and there are three or four men, wearing full length knee-top waders, actually searching in the water near the riverbank. On the towpath a uniformed POLICE SERGEANT has charge of several police dogs.

Suddenly one of the men wearing waders strikes something in the water and lifts his arm in obvious excitement. He calls across to his colleagues.

MAN: (*Shouting*) Here we are!
The MAN in the river stoops down, takes hold of something and begins to lift the object out of the water.

CUT TO: *A group of people – plain and uniformed police – near the bank of the river. Two or three men come into view, climbing up the bank from the river, and carrying the wet and inert body of a dead girl.*

CUT TO: *An ambulance is parked on the grass edge of the riverbank. A group of people – plain and uniformed police, ambulance attendants etc. – are standing very close to the ambulance. Two men appear from the lower bank of the river carrying a stretcher; the figure on the stretcher is covered by a sheet. DR SHELDON, carrying his medical bag, walks by the side of the two attendants. The stretcher bearers cross towards the ambulance and the stretcher is placed inside. The doors of the ambulance are closed.*

CUT TO: A Road near the river.
SERGEANT BRODERICK is standing alone, on the side of the road, waiting the arrival of a police car which can be seen in the distance approaching from the main road.

The police car brakes to a standstill near SERGEANT BRODERICK. There are two uniformed men in the front of the car. BRODERICK opens the door and gets into the back of the car.

CUT TO: Inside the Police Car.
BRODERICK is sitting down next to INSPECTOR FORD.
FORD: (*A shade tense*) I was at Windsor when your message came through. What's happened?

BRODERICK extracts his wallet and takes out a ten shilling note.
BRODERICK: (*Grimly*) I owe you ten shillings, Mike.
BRODERICK hands FORD the ten shilling note.

END OF EPISODE THREE

EPISODE FOUR

OPEN TO: A Road near the river.

SERGEANT BRODERICK is standing alone, on the side of the road, waiting the arrival of a police car which can be seen in the distance approaching from the main road.

The police car brakes to a standstill near SERGEANT BRODERICK. There are two uniformed men in the front of the car. BRODERICK opens the door and gets into the back of the car.

CUT TO: Inside the Police Car.

BRODERICK is sitting down next to INSPECTOR FORD.

FORD: (*A shade tense*) I was at Windsor when your message came through. What's happened?

BRODERICK extracts his wallet and takes out a ten shilling note.

BRODERICK: (*Grimly*) I owe you ten shillings, Mike.

BRODERICK hands FORD the ten shilling note.

FORD: (*Taking the note*) You've found Billie Reynolds?

BRODERICK: Yes.

FORD: Where?

BRODERICK: Fallow End. The body was in the river about ten yards from the bank.

FORD: What did Dr Jennings say?

BRODERICK: Jennings is away, Sheldon's P.D. for the next two weeks.

FORD: (*Surprised*) Oh, is he?

BRODERICK: Sheldon said he didn't want to commit himself but …

FORD: Oh, my God, has he started …

BRODERICK: … But he thought the body had been in the water for some little time.

FORD: What did he mean – some little time?

BRODERICK: He said a week or ten days, perhaps even longer.

103

FORD: (*Significantly*) It's ten days since she saw Henderson.

BRODERICK: Yes, I know it is. (*Shaking his head*) But surely Henderson couldn't have done this? What possible motive could he have for murdering Billie Reynolds?

FORD: (*Quietly*) You know the motive as well as I do. She saw Henderson the night he brought Rocello back to the houseboat.

BRODERICK: Yes …

FORD: I'll see Henderson again and I'll talk to Merson. You break the news to Chris Reynolds.

BRODERICK: (*Thoughtfully*) I wonder how he's going to take this …

FORD leans forward and speaks to the driver who is out of view.

FORD: (*To driver*) Drive us back to Medlow, George.

CUT TO: *The Police Car turns round and returns along the country lane towards the main road.*

CUT TO: The Local Police Station at Medlow.

The police car is parked outside. DAVID HENDERSON can be seen walking down the road towards the police station. A uniformed policeman comes out of the station and gets into the police car. HENDERSON reaches the station and turns into the main entrance.

CUT TO: INSPECTOR FORD's Office.

FORD is questioning RALPH MERSON who is obviously worried and on edge.

MERSON: … But it might be suicide, Inspector. I just don't see how you can be so sure that it isn't. Unless of course you're keeping something back from me.

FORD:	There's got to be a motive, Mr Merson – even for suicide.
MERSON:	Yes, I know that, but –
FORD:	Can you suggest a motive? Can you suggest why Miss Reynolds should have committed suicide?
MERSON:	No, on the other hand I can't suggest why she should have been murdered.
FORD:	(*After a moment*) Mr Merson, tell me: do you know a man called Henderson – David Henderson?
MERSON:	David Henderson? No, I don't think so.
FORD:	He's a Housemaster at Buckingham College.
MERSON:	(*Shaking his head*) No, I don't think I've ever heard of him.
FORD:	Miss Reynolds didn't mention the name to you at any time?
MERSON:	If she did I certainly can't recall it.

FORD nods.

FORD:	That note, Mr Merson – the one that came with the earring.
MERSON:	Yes?
FORD:	You've still no idea who sent it to you?
MERSON:	Not the slightest – but whoever sent it obviously knew what he was talking about. He knew that Billie was dead.
FORD:	(*Watching MERSON; nodding, quietly*) Yes.
MERSON:	(*Puzzled*) Why did you ask me about this man Henderson – was he a friend of Billie's?
FORD:	We believe so.
MERSON:	(*A sudden thought*) Was it Henderson that sent me the note?
FORD:	We don't know. We don't know who sent it. (*Changing the subject*) You say the last time you saw Miss Reynolds was just over a week ago?

105

MERSON: (*Faintly irritated*) It was the night I stayed with her; the night the Italian was brought back to the houseboat.

FORD: Was Miss Reynolds quite cheerful that night or did she seem perturbed in any way?

MERSON: (*Hesitant*) She seemed a little uneasy I thought, but it may have been my imagination.

FORD: Did you have a row with her, by any chance?

MERSON: Certainly not.

FORD: You're sure?

MERSON: I'm quite sure.

FORD: (*Looking at MERSON*) Now's the time to be perfectly frank with me, Mr Merson. If there's anything at the back of your mind, let's hear about it.

MERSON: There's nothing at the back of my mind and I always have been perfectly frank with you, Inspector! Dash it all, if it hadn't been for me you wouldn't have found the body.

FORD: Has Miss Reynolds any other 'boyfriends', besides yourself I mean?

MERSON: (*Annoyed*) You've asked me that question before. I've told you: I don't know.

FORD: (*Quite simply; unperturbed*) And you don't know who murdered her?

MERSON: Of course I don't know who murdered her! If I knew I should tell you!

PC SANDERS enters.

FORD: (*To SANDERS*) Yes – what is it?

SANDERS: The gentleman you're expecting has arrived, sir.

FORD: (*Nodding*) All right – I'll ring. Oh, has Dr Sheldon's report come through yet?

SANDERS: Not yet, sir.

FORD: Let me have it the moment it arrives.

SANDERS nods and goes out.

MERSON: Inspector, is there going to be a lot of publicity over this business?

FORD: It'll be in the newspapers, if that's what you mean.

MERSON: Will I be mentioned, do you think?

FORD: That rather depends …

MERSON: On what?

FORD: On the way things turn out. (*Suddenly, holding out his hand*) Thank you for calling, sir.

MERSON: Look, Inspector, the first time I saw you you gave me your word that I wouldn't be mixed up in anything. Now you tell me that …

FORD: (*Interrupting MERSON*) I didn't do anything of the kind, sir. Besides the situation's changed. Miss Reynolds is dead.

MERSON: (*Irritated and faintly exasperated*) Yes, I know, but don't you understand my wife doesn't know anything about Billie Reynolds. When she learns that I was a friend of hers it's going to be a dreadful shock.

FORD: (*With a shrug*) You could have thought of that earlier, Mr Merson.

FORD presses the button on his desk and turns towards the window.

FORD: (*His back to MERSON*) Sanders will see you out.

MERSON looks at FORD for a moment, is about to say something, then changes his mind and goes out. After a moment FORD turns from the window and sits at his desk. He picks up a document and is reading it when the door opens and HENDERSON enters.

FORD: (*Looking up*) Come in, Mr Henderson. (*Indicates a chair facing his desk*) Sit down, sir.

107

HENDERSON looks at FORD then sits down. FORD continues reading his report then finally puts it down and looks at HENDERSON.

FORD: (*Quietly*) Do you know why I sent for you?

HENDERSON: (*Smiling*) Presumably because you want to ask me some more questions. You seem to be making quite a habit of it, Inspector.

FORD: The last time I saw you I questioned you about Billie Reynolds.

HENDERSON: You did. You did, indeed.

FORD: I told you she'd disappeared.

HENDERSON: That's right.

FORD: You said you hadn't the slightest idea where she was.

HENDERSON: I still haven't.

FORD: (*After a moment*) Do you know a man called Merson – Ralph Merson?

HENDERSON: No.

FORD: Did you send him a note, together with an earring – an earring belonging to Billie Reynolds?

HENDERSON: Now don't be stupid, Inspector! I've just told you, I don't know the man. (*Amused*) In any case, why should I send him an earring belonging to Miss Reynolds? And what on earth would I be doing with one of her earrings anyway?

FORD: (*Quietly; watching HENDERSON's reaction*) I don't believe you, Henderson. I don't believe a word you're saying.

HENDERSON: What do you mean?

FORD: You sent Merson a note. It was in your handwriting. Now the point is – why did you send it? Did you think the note would throw

	suspicion on to him? Or did you send it simply because …
HENDERSON:	(*A shade angry*) I've told you, I didn't send Merson a note. And what do you mean – throw suspicion on to him? Has something happened to Billie Reynolds?
FORD:	She's dead.
HENDERSON:	(*Surprised*) Dead? How do you mean she's dead?
FORD:	We picked her body out of the river, just over three hours ago. She was murdered.

HENDERSON is apparently staggered.

HENDERSON:	Good God … (*He stares at FORD; tensely*) What happened? How was she murdered?
FORD:	We don't know. We haven't had the doctor's report yet.
HENDERSON:	(*A note of urgency*) You don't need a doctor's report! You saw the girl. What happened? How was she murdered?

FORD looks at HENDERSON for a moment.

FORD:	Supposing you tell me, Mr Henderson.
HENDERSON:	What are you suggesting? Do you think I murdered her?

FORD leans forward across the desk.

FORD:	Billie Reynolds called to see you ten days ago and it's my bet she didn't call to talk about …
HENDERSON:	(*Interrupting FORD*) I told you why she called! The school had had trouble with her and she was worried because we'd put the river out of bounds. If you don't believe my story you can contact the school …
FORD:	I've already done that.
HENDERSON:	Well?
FORD:	Your story's true – up to a point.

HENDERSON: Well, that's something anyway …

FORD: … But beyond that point I just don't believe you.

HENDERSON: (*A moment; quietly*) I'm sorry to hear you say that, Inspector.

FORD: I'm sorry to have to say it, sir.

HENDERSON: (*A moment*) What is it you don't believe?

FORD: I don't believe Miss Reynolds was concerned about the boys not being able to use the river. It's my bet she called to see you about something quite different.

HENDERSON: What – for instance?

FORD: I think Miss Reynolds was blackmailing you. I think she knew about your relationship with Rocello and she threatened to tell the police about it.

HENDERSON: But I didn't know Rocello. I never met the man – I've already told you that.

FORD: (*Shaking his head*) You were seen leaving the houseboat, sir. Miss Walters saw you.

HENDERSON: (*No longer quite so tense; in control of himself*) Miss Walters made a mistake – and if you think I murdered Billie Reynolds you're making a mistake too, Inspector.

PC SANDERS enters; he carries a sheet of foolscap paper which he places on the desk in front of the INSPECTOR.

SANDERS: Dr Sheldon's report, sir. It's just arrived.

FORD: Thank you. (*Stopping SANDERS*) Wait a moment …

FORD looks at the sheet of foolscap; HENDERSON watches him.

A pause.

HENDERSON: How was she murdered?

FORD ignores the question and continues reading the report; eventually he looks up.

FORD: (*To SANDERS*) Mr Henderson's leaving. You can show him out.

HENDERSON rises, looks across at SANDERS, then at FORD, and then down at the sheet of foolscap on FORD's desk. The INSPECTOR is looking at the report again.

CUT TO: The Living Room of DR SHELDON's House.

HENDERSON enters followed by JUDY, the parlourmaid. He looks worried and unusually serious.

JUDY: I'm afraid Dr Sheldon's out, sir.

HENDERSON: (*Nodding*) I'll wait.

JUDY: I don't know what time he's expected back, sir.

HENDERSON: That's all right.

JUDY: I believe he had to go into Maidenhead.

HENDERSON: (*With a smile*) I'll wait, Judy. Is Miss Walters in?

JUDY: She was a little while ago. She's probably in the garden, sir.

HENDERSON stops JUDY from crossing over to the French windows.

HENDERSON: It's all right, don't trouble Miss Walters. Just let me know when Dr Sheldon arrives.

JUDY: (*Hesitantly*) Yes, sir. Is there anything I can get you, Mr Henderson?

HENDERSON: No, thank you.

JUDY goes out. HENDERSON crosses, looks out of the French windows, and then returns to the centre of the room. He stands for a moment by the telephone then suddenly takes a notebook out of his pocket, consults it, glances at his watch, then picks up the telephone receiver.

HENDERSON: (*On the telephone*) Flaxman one – nine –
                eight – four, please.

OPERATOR's VOICE: One – nine – eight- four?

HENDERSON: Yes, please.

HENDERSON looks towards the French windows. After a
moment we hear the number ringing out. There is a long pause
and then we hear the receiver being lifted at the other end.

HENDERSON: (*On the telephone*) Cooper?

COOPER's VOICE: (*On the other end of the line*) Yes.

HENDERSON: This is Henderson.

COOPER: (*Pleasantly*) Oh, hello, Henderson. I've been
                expecting to hear from you.

HENDERSON: (*A note of tenseness in his voice*) Cooper,
                listen. I've just left Ford. They've found
                Billie Reynolds.

COOPER: (*Quietly*) Yes, I know.

HENDERSON: (*Surprised*) You know?

HENDERSON looks towards the French windows; he has
obviously heard someone approaching.

COOPER: Yes. I intended to phone you but
                unfortunately …

HENDERSON: (*Quickly; interrupting*) I can't talk now. I'll
                ring you back in an hour.

HENDERSON replaces the receiver and turns towards the
French windows as KATHERINE WALTERS enters.

KATHERINE: (*Surprised*) Oh, hello, Mr Henderson! I didn't
                know you were here.

HENDERSON: I wanted to see your uncle but I understand
                he's out.

KATHERINE: Yes, he is I'm afraid. I don't know what time
                he'll be back. Didn't Judy tell you that?

HENDERSON: Yes, she did but I insisted on waiting.

KATHERINE: Oh, I see.

There is a slightly uncomfortable pause for KATHERINE.

KATHERINE:	Has your shoulder been troubling you again?
HENDERSON:	My shoulder? Oh, no. No, it's perfectly all right now, thank you.
KATHERINE:	(*Crossing towards the door*) Well, if you'll excuse me ...
HENDERSON:	(*Stopping KATHERINE*) Miss Walters ...
KATHERINE:	(*Turning*) Yes?
HENDERSON:	Have you seen your uncle this afternoon?
KATHERINE:	Yes, I saw him about an hour ago.
HENDERSON:	Did he tell you about Miss Reynolds – Billie Reynolds?
KATHERINE:	Is that the girl that disappeared – the girl they found in the river?
HENDERSON:	Yes.
KATHERINE:	(*Nodding*) He said she'd been murdered.
HENDERSON:	How was she murdered – do you know?
KATHERINE:	(*Surprised by the question*) No, I'm sorry I don't.
HENDERSON:	Didn't your uncle tell you?
KATHERINE:	I'm afraid Dr Sheldon doesn't discuss his patients with me.
HENDERSON:	Was Miss Reynolds a patient of his then?
KATHERINE:	She may have been, I'm not sure. The Police Surgeon – Doctor Jennings – is away at the moment and that's why my uncle was called in.
HENDERSON:	Yes, I know.
KATHERINE:	(*Curious*) Is that why you wanted to see my uncle, because of what's happened to Miss Reynolds?
HENDERSON:	Yes. I want to know how she was murdered.
KATHERINE:	Was Billie Reynolds a friend of yours then?
HENDERSON:	No.
KATHERINE:	Then why are you interested in her?

113

HENDERSON:	(*Smiling*) For a number of reasons, Miss Walters. But I'll give you just one. The police think I murdered her.
KATHERINE:	(*Looking at HENDERSON, quite simply*) And did you?
HENDERSON:	No. Strange though it may seem, I'm not in the habit of murdering people.
KATHERINE:	Then why should the police suspect you?
HENDERSON:	They think that this murder may be tied up with the previous one – the Italian.
KATHERINE:	Oh, I see.
HENDERSON:	(*Looking at KATHERINE*) I wonder if you do see, Miss Walters.
KATHERINE:	Look, Mr Henderson, do you mind if I ask you a very frank question?
HENDERSON:	Not at all.
KATHERINE:	You remember the day you came here – to see my uncle – because your shoulder was hurting you?
HENDERSON:	Yes?
KATHERINE:	Was your shoulder hurting you, or was it just an excuse to come here?
HENDERSON:	(*A moment*) It was just an excuse. I knew that you'd reported me to the police and I wanted to take a good look at you.
KATHERINE:	That's not what you said at the time. You said that you knew that someone had reported you but you didn't know who that someone was.
HENDERSON:	I didn't wish to embarrass you.
KATHERINE:	(*Quietly*) It <u>was</u> you I saw that afternoon, wasn't it?
HENDERSON:	(*Facing KATHERINE; shaking his head*) No.

KATHERINE: (*Surprised by the denial*) But it was! I saw you – I saw you quite distinctly. I saw you leave the houseboat and get into the car.

HENDERSON: (*Shaking his head*) It might have been someone who looked like me – it obviously was – but it wasn't me, Miss Walters.

KATHERINE stares at HENDERSON then moves away; she obviously doesn't believe him. HENDERSON looks at her; he is a shade worried. DR SHELDON enters from the hall; he carries his medical bag and a black homburg hat.

SHELDON: (*To HENDERSON*) Hello, Henderson! I hope you haven't been waiting long?

HENDERSON: No …

SHELDON: (*To KATHERINE*) Did Nurse Steele telephone?

KATHERINE: Yes. Judy took the call, there's a message on your desk.

SHELDON: Oh, good.

KATHERINE: Would you like a cup of tea?

SHELDON: Er – later, Katherine.

KATHERINE looks at HENDERSON and then goes out.

SHELDON: (*To HENDERSON; putting his bag down on the settee*) Did you have an appointment?

HENDERSON: No, I'm afraid I didn't, but I won't keep you a minute, doctor. It's just that … (*He hesitates*)

SHELDON: Shall we go into my consulting room?

HENDERSON: No, no, there's no need. It's just that – I'd like some information from you. (*Smiling*) That is, of course, if you've no objection.

SHELDON: What kind of information?

HENDERSON: Inspector Ford told me about Miss Reynolds. He said it was you that examined the body.

SHELDON: That's right. Dr Jennings is away.

HENDERSON: How did she die, exactly?

115

SHELDON: (*Surprised by the question*) Miss Reynolds?
HENDERSON: Yes.
SHELDON: She was murdered.
HENDERSON: Yes, I know that, but how?
SHELDON: (*Quietly; watching HENDERSON*) You say
                you've seen Inspector Ford?
HENDERSON: (*Pleasantly; disarming*) Yes, I've just left
                him. It was Ford that told me about the
                murder.
SHELDON: Then why didn't you ask Inspector Ford your
                question?
HENDERSON: (*Unruffled; still pleasant*) Well, I thought
                you'd know more about it, that's all. You're
                the doctor.
SHELDON: I've made my report; so far as I'm concerned
                it's confidential. If you've got any questions
                to ask, ask Inspector Ford.
HENDERSON smiles; he appears quite unperturbed.
HENDERSON: All right, doctor. Sorry to have bothered you.
HENDERSON crosses to the door.
SHELDON: How's your shoulder, Mr Henderson?
HENDERSON: (*Turning*) Oh, it's very much better. I've even
                started to play tennis again. I think your
                ointment did the trick.
SHELDON: (*Nodding*) I thought it would.
*HENDERSON smiles and goes out. SHELDON stands watching
him.*

CUT TO: DAVID HENDERSON's Study. Afternoon.
*CHRIS REYNOLDS is sitting in an armchair casually filing his
nails with a pocket nailfile. MRS WILLIAMS enters, she looks at
CHRIS with obvious annoyance.*
MRS WILLIAMS: Mr Henderson's just arrived.

CHRIS:	(*Not looking up*) Well, there you are, Ma. It 'asn't been long 'as it?
MRS WILLIAMS:	You've been here over an hour.
CHRIS:	(*Looking up; grinning*) I've been very 'appy. Very 'appy.
MRS WILLIAMS:	What is it you want with Mr Henderson anyway?
CHRIS:	I've told you, it's none o' your business. (*He rises; puts the file in his pocket*) Now just you run along, Maralyn, there's a good girl. (*Jerks his head*) Go on, 'op it!

HENDERSON enters from his interview with DR SHELDON. He stops dead on seeing CHRIS REYNOLDS.

HENDERSON:	Hello – who are you? What do you want?
CHRIS:	Are you Henderson?
HENDERSON:	Yes?
CHRIS:	(*Holding out his hand; grinning*) Glad to meet you. Reynolds is the name. Chris Reynolds.
MRS WILLIAMS:	(*To HENDERSON*) I'm sorry, Mr Henderson, but he insisted on waiting. He's been here over an hour.
HENDERSON:	(*Looking at REYNOLDS; quietly, ignoring the outstretched hand*) Yes, all right, Mrs Williams – you can go.

MRS WILLIAMS looks across at CHRIS and then goes out.

HENDERSON:	Did you say your name was Reynolds?
CHRIS:	Christopher Hubert Reynolds, Esq. My friends call me Chris.
HENDERSON:	Was Miss – Billie Reynolds a relation of yours?
CHRIS:	(*Nodding*) Sure. She was my sister.
HENDERSON:	Oh, I didn't realise … I'm sorry, Reynolds – about your sister, I mean.

117

CHRIS: Yes, it's sad, isn't it? Very, very sad. Mind
                    you I always said she'd come to a sticky
                    end. (*He smiles at HENDERSON*) You
                    can't play with fire an' not get burnt, can
                    you, Mr Henderson? (*His expression
                    changes slightly*) Or can you?
HENDERSON: (*Quietly; facing him*) What is it you want?
CHRIS: Well, I just wanted to have a little chat,
                    that's all. I knew you was a friend of
                    Billie's an' I felt a bit sentimental. You
                    know how it is on these occasions.
HENDERSON: (*Same tone*) What is it you want?
CHRIS: You've said that before 'an I've told you, I
                    don't want anything. I just want to have a
                    little chat that's all.

HENDERSON sits on the arm of the settee.

HENDERSON: Who told you I was a friend of your sister?
CHRIS: Billie did – she was very nice about you.
                    She said Mr Henderson's different, Chris –
                    he's such a gentleman. Very partial to the
                    public-school type was my sister. Funny
                    really, considering.
HENDERSON: Look, Reynolds, please don't think I'm
                    rude but there seems to be some mistake. I
                    only met your sister once and that was
                    twelve months ago.
CHRIS: Really? Don't you count the time she
                    came here then?
HENDERSON: (*Cautiously*) When was that?
CHRIS: Supposing you tell me? (*He smiles and
                    rises*) When was it, chum – just over a
                    week ago?

A pause.

118

HENDERSON:	(*Quite simply*) Are you trying to blackmail me?
CHRIS:	Blackmail you? Why should I want to blackmail you? You was a friend of Billie's, Mr Henderson. Any friend of Billie's is a friend of mine. No, I feel very friendly disposed towards you if you must know. Very friendly.

HENDERSON leans forward and looks at CHRIS.

HENDERSON:	I've met your type before, Reynolds. You're up to something. Now what is it?
CHRIS:	(*Grinning at HENDERSON*) Can you play chess?

To CHRIS's complete amazement HENDERSON suddenly springs forward and grabs him by the lapel of his jacket. HENDERSON's manner is tense and tough; he holds Chris in a vice-like grip.

HENDERSON:	I said: What is it?

CHRIS is terrified, almost repulsed by HENDERSON's toughness, but he puts on a front and gradually releases himself. He shakes himself, walks away from HENDERSON, then suddenly turns.

CHRIS:	(*Angrily*) My sister kept a diary. A nice, chatty, day-to-day diary. I found it this morning at the bottom of an old chest of drawers. (*He points at HENDERSON*) You're in that diary, chummy – you an' a 'ell of a lot of other people!
HENDERSON:	Well?
CHRIS:	Well, use your imagination, Teacher!
HENDERSON:	(*After a moment*) Where is this diary?
CHRIS:	Where d'you think? (*He walks towards HENDERSON*) D'you think I'd carry it around with me?

HENDERSON: (*Quietly; not unfriendly*) Reynolds, I'm
               serious – where is it?

CHRIS faces HENDERSON; he is still angry with him.

CHRIS: (*Almost a threat*) How much?

HENDERSON: (*Laughing; almost pleasant in manner*) What
               d'you mean – how much?

CHRIS: (*Nastily; on the verge of losing his temper*)
               You know what I mean! That diary's worth
               lolly – a packet o' lolly. How much?

HENDERSON: (*A shrug; smiling*) How can I tell you what
               it's worth when I haven't seen it?

*CHRIS is not sure of HENDERSON; he looks at him for a
moment.*

CHRIS: All right, chummy – you can see it tonight.
               Meet me at the houseboat – seven o'clock.

HENDERSON: (*Quite friendly*) Now wait a minute! Has
               anyone else seen this diary? Have you shown
               it to anyone?

CHRIS: (*Shaking his head*) What do you take me for?

HENDERSON: Are you sure?

CHRIS: 'Course I'm sure.

A pause.

HENDERSON: All right, seven o'clock.

*CHRIS looks at HENDERSON, then crosses towards the door.
He stops and turns.*

CHRIS: And don't ever do that again, Mr Henderson –
               ever.

HENDERSON: What do you mean?

CHRIS: (*Hunching his shoulders; almost a gesture of
               distaste*) Don't get hold of me like that see; I
               don't like it. Always been allergic to that kind
               'o thing. Don't like it at all. Besides – (*He
               takes a flick knife out of his pocket and*

120

quickly – expertly – flicks open the blade) …
You took an awful risk.

CHRIS looks down at the knife; then up at HENDERSON. He forces a smile and then turns and goes out. HENDERSON watches the door then suddenly crosses to the table and picks up the telephone receiver.

OPERATOR: (*On the other end of the phone*) Number, please?

HENDERSON: (*Quickly; tensely*) Get me Flaxman one – nine – eight – four …

CUT TO: INSPECTOR FORD's Office. The same afternoon.
FORD is sitting at his desk reading a report. The door opens and PC SANDERS enters.

FORD: (*Looking up; irritable*) What is it?

SANDERS: There's a Mr Craven would like to see you. It's the third time he's called, sir.

FORD: He's a newspaper man. I don't want to see him. Get rid of him.

SANDERS: Er – yes, sir.

FORD: Has Miss Rocello arrived?

SANDERS: Not yet, sir.

FORD: Show her in the moment she gets here – don't keep her waiting.

SANDERS: Yes, sir.

BRODERICK enters as SANDERS goes out.

BRODERICK: (*To FORD*) Young Craven's outside.

FORD: (*Putting down the report*) Yes, I know. Bob, where the Dickens have you been all day?

BRODERICK: I went over to Slough to interview a woman who was supposed to be a friend of Billie Reynolds. It turned out she'd never even seen her.

121

FORD: (*Smiling*) That sounds like a bum steer. Who gave you that one?

BRODERICK: Chris Reynolds.

FORD: Oh, yes. What about Chris Reynolds? Did you break the news to him?

BRODERICK: He was heartbroken. I don't think! I might have been talking about a stranger. He didn't bat an eyelid.

FORD: Wasn't he surprised?

BRODERICK: No. (*With sarcasm*) Apparently he always knew his sister would come to a sticky end.

FORD: He's a charmer, that young man. A real charmer.

BRODERICK: Yes, but I'm not so sure he doesn't know a great deal more about this business than we think he does.

FORD: (*Interested*) Why do you say that?

BRODERICK: It's just a hunch.

FORD: (*Nodding*) Have another talk to Reynolds. Drop in on him tonight sometime, he won't be expecting you.

BRODERICK: He wasn't expecting me this morning, but it didn't seem to worry him. (*He sits on the arm of the chair facing the desk*) Mike, has a Miss Rocello phoned you?

FORD: Yes, she called about an hour ago. (*He looks at his watch*) I'm seeing her at six o'clock.

BRODERICK: She's Paul Rocello's sister; she arrived in Medlow this afternoon. Apparently she's staying at The White Hart.

FORD: (*Nodding; curious*) Yes, I know – but how did you know?

BRODERICK: I'm a detective. (*Laughing*) I bumped into
                  Ted Crawford, the head porter, he tipped me
                  off. What's she doing in Medlow?
FORD: She didn't say. She just told me who she was
                  and said she wanted to see me.
BRODERICK: According to Ted she's quite a dish.
FORD: I don't know what you mean, Sergeant.
PC SANDERS enters.
SANDERS: (*To FORD*) Miss Rocello, sir.
MARIA ROCELLO comes into the office. She is an attractive,
well-dressed girl in the late twenties. SANDERS goes out.
BRODERICK rises from the chair.
FORD: (*Pleasantly*) Miss Rocello? I'm Detective
                  Inspector Ford. (*Shakes hands*) This is
                  Detective Sergeant Broderick.
BRODERICK shakes hands with MARIA and indicates his chair.
MARIA: How do you do? It's so very kind of you to
                  see me at such short notice.
BRODERICK: Do sit down, Miss Rocello.
BRODERICK takes out his cigarette case.
BRODERICK: May I offer you a cigarette?
MARIA: No. No, thank you.
FORD gives BRODERICK a look, as much to say 'Switch off the
charm, Bob'.
FORD: (*Sitting behind the desk*) You said over the
                  telephone that you'd just arrived from Italy,
                  Miss Rocello.
MARIA: Yes. I left Milan this morning, at seven
                  o'clock.
FORD: Why did you come to Medlow? If it's
                  information you want surely Scotland Yard
                  would have been the best place for you to …
MARIA: I went to Scotland Yard. I saw Superintendent
                  Harringday – (*FORD nods*). He told me you

123

	were in charge of the case. (*A shade tense*) Inspector Ford, why was my brother murdered?
FORD:	I'm afraid we don't know why. We're still pursuing our investigations, Miss Rocello.
MARIA:	But you must have some – what is the word? – some idea, some understanding as to why this terrible thing happened?
BRODERICK:	(*Quietly*) Have you any idea why it happened, Miss Rocello?
MARIA:	(*Turning to BRODERICK*) Me? Why, no! When I heard the news I could hardly believe it. I thought at first there had been some mistake. Then a friend of mine showed me an English newspaper and I knew then that – that there had been no mistake after all.
FORD:	Miss Rocello, tell me about this man Cooper. Was he a very good friend of your brother?
MARIA:	They seemed to be good friends. Paul introduced me to him about two years ago when they were in Naples together working on some project or other. Last year both of them came to Florence and stayed with me for three or four days. I liked Mr Cooper, he seemed a very nice man.
BRODERICK:	You say, Cooper and your brother were working together?
MARIA:	Yes, but I do not know what on. Is that right – what on?
BRODERICK:	(*Smiling*) Yes, that's right.
FORD is studying MARIA as she speaks to BRODERICK.	
MARIA:	Paul – my brother – was with an engineering firm called Galvari and Schuster, they had their headquarters in Naples.

124

BRODERICK:	And Mr Cooper – was he with Galvari and Schuster?
MARIA:	Yes, I think he was an associate of theirs, I'm not sure.
BRODERICK:	Did you know that Cooper has a houseboat and that your brother was going to stay on it?
MARIA:	No, I thought he'd an apartment in London – in Mayfair – that's where Paul told me he was going to stay.
FORD:	(*Quietly*) You know of course that Cooper's disappeared, that we've been unable to trace him?
MARIA:	(*Nodding*) Superintendent Harringday told me and it was in one of your newspapers.

FORD nods, looks at MARIA and then opens a drawer in his desk and takes out the wristlet watch which was placed on the dead man's wrist by DAVID HENDERSON.

FORD:	Miss Rocello, I'd like you to take a look at this watch. (*He holds up the watch so that the dial faces MARIA*) Have you seen it before?
MARIA:	(*Unhesitatingly*) But of course! It's Paul's!
FORD:	There's an inscription on the back.
MARIA:	That's right. It's our family – what do you call it in this country, motto? Suavitor in modo, fortiter in re.
FORD:	Gentle in the manner but vigorous in the deed.
MARIA:	(*Smiling slightly*) That's right, Inspector.

FORD looks at MARIA then puts the watch down on the desk.

FORD:	Miss Rocello, did you brother ever mention a man called Henderson?
MARIA:	Henderson?
FORD:	Yes, David Henderson.
MARIA:	No.

FORD:	You're sure?
MARIA:	Yes, I'm quite sure.
FORD:	You've never heard the name before?
MARIA:	(*Puzzled*) No, I'm afraid I haven't. Who is this David Henderson?

FORD glances across at BRODERICK and hesitates.

BRODERICK:	He's a schoolmaster at a public school near Medlow. We think he might be concerned, in some way or other, with the death of your brother.
MARIA:	What do you mean – concerned? (*Tensely*) Did he murder my brother?
FORD:	(*Quietly*) We don't know who murdered your brother, Miss Rocello.
MARIA:	(*Quickly; still a shade tense*) But you think that this man Henderson …
FORD:	(*With a note of authority*) We're not sure about Henderson, not yet. We're still – making inquiries.

MARIA looks at FORD then at BRODERICK.

MARIA:	(*Softly; nodding*) I see.
BRODERICK:	I assure you, we're doing everything we can. We're just as anxious to find the murderer as you are, Miss Rocello.
FORD:	How long do you propose staying in Medlow?
MARIA:	I shall stay until something happens. Until you make an arrest or decide that the case is over.
FORD:	(*Faintly concerned*) But that may be a very long time. There's no reason why you should stay, you know. Not now. We can always get in touch with you.
MARIA:	I shall stay – for a time at any rate.

FORD rises and comes round the desk.

FORD: All right, Miss Rocello. If you want us, you know where we are. And thank you for calling.

MARIA: (*Rising*) Thank you, Inspector.

FORD: Oh – if anyone contacts you by any chance, let me know.

MARIA: But I don't know anyone in Medlow, who would … Oh, you mean, newspaper people – reporters?

FORD: (*Shaking hands with her*) I mean anyone. Whoever contacts you – let me know.

MARIA: (*Puzzled*) Yes, of course.

BRODERICK takes hold of MARIA's arm and leads her towards the door. FORD turns and thoughtfully picks up the watch from the desk. The dial on the watch registers that the time is six fifteen.

CUT TO: BILLIE's Cabin on the houseboat Shangri La.

The cuckoo clock on the wall registers that it is twenty past seven. The cabin is now in distinct disorder. The table overturned; chairs scattered; the settee pushed to one side. It looks as if a struggle has taken place and the cabin has been the loser.

There is a knock on the main door of the cabin and after a moment or two the knock is repeated. There is a pause then the door opens and ROBIN CRAVEN enters. He stands in the doorway staring at the cabin in astonishment. He slowly enters and looks round the cabin; after a moment he crosses to the door on the left.

CRAVEN: (*Calling*) Anybody at home?

CRAVEN opens the door to the left and peers into the adjoining cabin.

CRAVEN: (*Calling into the adjoining cabin*) Hello, there! Anybody at home?

The adjoining cabin is obviously deserted and CRAVEN closes the door and returns to the centre of the main cabin. He takes off his hat, obviously bewildered, suddenly he hears something and turns sharply towards the main door. DETECTIVE SERGEANT BRODERICK is standing in the doorway.

BRODERICK: Good evening, Mr Craven! This is a pleasant surprise.

CRAVEN: (*Without thinking*) What are you doing here?

BRODERICK: What's more to the point – what are you doing here?

BRODERICK enters the cabin; looks around him.

CRAVEN: I came to see Chris Reynolds.

BRODERICK: So did I. (*Looking at the scattered furniture*) Two minds with but a single thought. Where is Reynolds?

CRAVEN: I don't know – he certainly isn't here.

BRODERICK: (*Indicating the cabin*) How did this happen?

CRAVEN: Don't ask me. I've only just arrived.

BRODERICK: Had you an appointment with Reynolds?

CRAVEN: No.

BRODERICK: What did you want to see him about?

CRAVEN: I'm writing an article on his sister and I want some information.

BRODERICK: (*A note of authority*) What kind of information?

CRAVEN: (*Smiling at BRODERICK*) I'd like to know who murdered her.

BRODERICK gives CRAVEN a look and then slowly walks round the cabin.

CRAVEN: (*Quietly*) Sergeant …

BRODERICK: (*Turning slightly*) Yes?

CRAVEN: Why Fallow End?

BRODERICK: (*Completely turning*) What do you mean?

128

CRAVEN: According to my information you found the body at Fallow End, about ten yards from the bank.

BRODERICK: Well?

CRAVEN: Well – why Fallow End? Who tipped you off?

BRODERICK: (*Irritable*) No one tipped us off.

CRAVEN: Someone must have done, otherwise you wouldn't have gone there. You're a pretty smart bunch down here, but you're not that smart.

BRODERICK looks at CRAVEN for a moment.

BRODERICK: (*Curious*) Craven, how well did you know Billie Reynolds?

CRAVEN: (*Surprised*) Me?

BRODERICK: Yes, you.

CRAVEN: I didn't know her – not to speak to at any rate.

BRODERICK: But you must have known her – a journalist, local correspondent – it's your job to know people.

CRAVEN: Nevertheless, I didn't know Miss Reynolds. As a matter of fact I only saw her twice. The first time was at a regatta, the second in a pub at Maidenhead.

BRODERICK: When was that?

CRAVEN: About two weeks ago.

BRODERICK: Was she alone?

CRAVEN: No, there was a man with her. A local chap – fellow I'd seen before.

BRODERICK: (*Both interested and curious*) Oh – who was it?

CRAVEN: It was you, Sergeant.

CRAVEN smiles at BRODERICK.

CUT TO: DAVID HENDERSON's Study.

The telephone is ringing. HENDERSON enters; he is wearing his hat and overcoat and appears a shade excited and breathless; a handkerchief is wrapped tightly round his right hand, covering a cut. He crosses the room and immediately picks up the telephone receiver.

HENDERSON: (*On the telephone*) Hello? Who is that?

COOPER: (*On the other end of the phone*) This is Cooper ...

HENDERSON takes a large diary out of his coat pocket and puts it on the table.

HENDERSON: It's all right, Cooper. I've got the diary, there's nothing to worry about.

COOPER: Good. (*Confidentially*) Now, Henderson, listen – there's another complication. Maria Rocello's arrived, she's in Medlow.

HENDERSON: (*Surprised*) In Medlow?

COOPER: Yes, she's staying at The White Hart.

HENDERSON: Well – what do you want me to do?

COOPER: I don't know, it's difficult. I'm leaving for Liverpool tomorrow morning.

HENDERSON: You remember what you suggested?

COOPER: (*Thoughtfully*) Yes ... (*Suddenly, a decision*) All right – take care of her. You know exactly what to do.

HENDERSON: (*Quietly*) Yes, I know. Goodnight, Cooper.

HENDERSON slowly replaces the receiver. He stands for a moment deep in thought then he picks up the diary, crosses to his desk, unlocks a drawer, places the diary in the drawer, relocks it, and then returns to the telephone. He picks up the local telephone directory; flicks through the pages, finds the number he wants and then lifts up the telephone receiver.

OPERATOR: (*On the other end of the phone*) Number, please?

HENDERSON: Medlow eight – one, please?

OPERATOR: Thank you …

After a moment we hear the number ringing out at the other end.
The receiver is lifted.

MAN: (*On the other end of the phone*) White Hart
                              Hotel …

HENDERSON: Could I speak to Miss Rocello, please? My
                              name is Henderson.

MAN: Miss Rocello? One moment, I'll see if she's
                              in.

HENDERSON holds the telephone receiver and waits. He looks
serious.

CUT TO: INSPECTOR FORD's Office. Early evening.

FORD is sitting at his desk smoking his pipe and writing a
routine report; he keeps referring to a foolscap document which
is on the desk. The telephone rings and the INSPECTOR reaches
out and picks up the receiver.

CUT TO: *MARIA ROCELLO is in a telephone box at The*
White Hart Hotel.

MARIA: (*A shade excited*) Inspector Ford?

FORD: Yes.

MARIA: This is Maria Rocello …

CUT TO: FORD's Office.

FORD: Oh, good evening, Miss Rocello.

MARIA: Inspector, I've just had a message from that
                              man you mentioned – David Henderson. He
                              wants to see me.

FORD: When?

MARIA: Tonight.

FORD: Where?

CUT TO: The Telephone Box.
MARIA: At his flat; he said anytime after nine o'clock.
FORD: What did you say?
MARIA: I asked him why he wanted to see me and he said
            he'd like to talk to me about my brother. What
            should I do, Inspector?

CUT TO: INSPECTOR FORD's Office.
FORD: (*A moment, then a sudden decision*) Keep the
            appointment. Take a taxi and leave the hotel about
            nine o'clock.
MARIA: Yes, all right.
FORD: Thank you for phoning. Oh, and Miss Rocello – if
            Henderson offers you a drink, don't accept it.

CUT TO: The Telephone Box.
MARIA slowly replaces the telephone receiver; she looks puzzled.

CUT TO: The entrance to Buckingham College. Night.
A police car, containing SERGEANT BRODERICK and several uniformed Police Officers, is parked near the main gate. Through the windscreen of the car we see MARIA ROCELLO arrive in a taxi; the taxi stops outside of the college and MARIA gets out.

CUT TO: HENDERSON's Study. Night.
HENDERSON enters with MARIA. She is wearing an attractive dress and a fur stole. HENDERSON takes her stole and places it on the back of the settee. HENDERSON is now wearing a dark suit and looks relaxed and completely at ease. There is a piece of sticking plaster on his hand in place of the handkerchief.

132

HENDERSON:	It's extremely nice of you to come, I appreciate it.
MARIA:	(*A shade nervous*) You said over the telephone there was something you'd like to tell me – about my brother.
HENDERSON:	I did. I did indeed. (*Smiling*) Do sit down, please.

MARIA hesitates then sits in one of the armchairs.

HENDERSON:	You must have been surprised when you got my phone call?
MARIA:	Yes, I was. I don't ever remember Paul – my brother – mentioning you, Mr Henderson.
HENDERSON:	(*Looking at MARIA; quietly*) No, I don't suppose you do.

There is a tiny pause.

MARIA looks round the room; taking stock of her surroundings.

HENDERSON:	(*Watching MARIA; smiling*) I'm a Housemaster at Buckingham College, hence the books. The college is the large building on the right – you probably saw it when you came through the gates.
MARIA:	(*Turning towards HENDERSON*) Yes, I believe I did.
HENDERSON:	(*A moment*) I was awfully sorry to hear about your brother. It was a dreadful shock to all of us.
MARIA:	(*Curious*) All of us?
HENDERSON:	Those who knew him.
MARIA:	How well did you know him, Mr Henderson?
HENDERSON:	(*After a momentary hesitation*) We met in Venice just after the war. I was in Italy for four years. What part of Italy do you come from, Miss Rocello?
MARIA:	From Florence.

133

HENDERSON: Ah, Florence! What was it Shelley said about
               …
MARIA: (*Deliberately interrupting HENDERSON*) Mr
               Henderson, how did you know I was in
               Medlow? How did you know I was staying at
               The White Hart?

*HENDERSON smiles at MARIA, then smiles and turns towards
the cupboard containing the drinks, decanters, etc. MARIA
watches HENDERSON preparing a drink.*

HENDERSON: (*His back towards MARIA*) A man called
               Craven told me. He's a journalist. He gets all
               the local gossip.
MARIA: Is that the man that wrote the article about my
               brother and Count Paragi – it was called
               'Murder of a Frogman'?
HENDERSON: Yes. Yes, that's the fellow. He's a curious
               young man. Quite talented in an odd sort of
               way.

*HENDERSON turns; crosses to MARIA with two glasses of
sherry in his hands.*

HENDERSON: You'd like a glass of sherry, I'm sure.
MARIA: No, thank you, I …
HENDERSON: (*Laughing; pleasantly*) Nonsense!

*HENDERSON hands MARIA one of the glasses and almost
without realising it, MARIA accepts it.*

HENDERSON: How long are you staying in Medlow?
MARIA: That depends.
HENDERSON: On what?
MARIA: On – a number of things.

There is a slight pause.

HENDERSON: Miss Rocello, correct me if I'm mistaken.
               You came to England for two reasons. One:
               because you want to know why your brother

134

	was murdered. Two: because you want to know who murdered him.
MARIA:	You are not mistaken. That's why I came to England – to Medlow.
HENDERSON:	Well, strange though it may seem, I can answer both questions.
MARIA:	(*Tensely; surprised*) You can?
HENDERSON:	Yes, I can.

HENDERSON smiles at MARIA, lifts his glass and sips his sherry.

HENDERSON:	(*Almost a friendly reproach; still smiling*) But you're not drinking your sherry, Miss Rocello.

MARIA looks at HENDERSON; hesitates, then looks down at the glass she is holding. She raises the glass slowly.

END OF EPISODE FOUR

EPISODE FIVE

OPEN TO: DAVID HENDERSON's Study. Night.

DAVID HENDERSON and MARIA ROCELLO are each holding a glass of sherry.

HENDERSON: How long are you staying in Medlow?

MARIA: That depends.

HENDERSON: On what?

MARIA: On – a number of things.

There is a slight pause.

HENDERSON: Miss Rocello, correct me if I'm mistaken. You came to England for two reasons. One: because you want to know why your brother was murdered. Two: because you want to know who murdered him.

MARIA: You are not mistaken. That's why I came to England – to Medlow.

HENDERSON: Well, strange though it may seem, I can answer both questions.

MARIA: (*Tensely; surprised*) You can?

HENDERSON: Yes, I can.

HENDERSON smiles at MARIA, lifts his glass and sips his sherry.

HENDERSON: (*Almost a friendly reproach; still smiling*) But you're not drinking your sherry, Miss Rocello.

MARIA looks at HENDERSON; hesitates, then looks down at the glass she is holding. She raises the glass slightly, as if about to drink, then suddenly puts the glass down on the table.

MARIA: (*Hesitantly, obviously a shade frightened*) Do you mind if I don't drink it? I'm not very fond of sherry.

HENDERSON: (*A shade puzzled; concerned*) No, of course not. I'm sorry, I should have realised that. May I get you something else? (*Smiling*) I have a bottle of Campari.

139

MARIA: (*Quite definite*) No. No, thank you.

HENDERSON *looks at MARIA for a moment and then down at the glass of sherry.*

HENDERSON: (*With a little smile*) Miss Rocello, did you speak to Inspector Ford after I telephoned you?

MARIA: (*Obviously lying*) Inspector Ford. Who … who is Inspector Ford?

HENDERSON: He's the gentleman you saw this evening, at six o'clock.

MARIA: I'm sorry, I don't know what you're talking about. I don't know anyone called Ford.

HENDERSON *looks at MARIA and smiles, puts his glass of sherry down on the table and then picks up MARIA's glass. He looks at her and then takes a long drink. After a moment he puts the glass down on the table.*

HENDERSON: Did you think I was trying to poison you?

MARIA: (*Embarrassed, with a little laugh*) No, no of course not.

HENDERSON: Miss Rocello, I'm a friend of your brother's – a very good friend, and because of that I'm going to give you a piece of advice.

MARIA: Well?

HENDERSON: Return to Italy – immediately.

MARIA: (*Defiantly*) Why should I do that?

HENDERSON: Because there's no reason for you to stay here.

MARIA: There's a very good reason. I want to know why my brother was murdered and who murdered him.

HENDERSON: And if I answer that question, will you return to Italy tomorrow morning?

MARIA: Mr Henderson, if you know who murdered my brother why don't you inform the police?

HENDERSON looks at MARIA for a moment.

HENDERSON: Are you serious about staying here, in Medlow?

MARIA: Yes, of course. I told the Inspector that … *(She hesitates, realising what she has said)*

HENDERSON: *(Smiling)* You told the Inspector, what?

MARIA: That I had every intention of staying here until the case was solved or closed.

HENDERSON looks MARIA. She looks determined.

HENDERSON: *(Quietly)* I see.

HENDERSON crosses to his desk, unlocks a drawer and takes out a photograph album. He takes a photograph out of the album and holds it up so that MARIA can see it.

HENDERSON: *(In an efficient, businesslike manner)* There are two people in this photograph. Tell me who they are.

MARIA is puzzled by HENDERSON's change of manner but she looks at the photograph.

MARIA: Well, one is my brother, the other is my fiancé, Carlo Marissa.

HENDERSON: When was the photograph taken?

MARIA: About two years ago.

HENDERSON: Where?

MARIA: At Sorrento. Outside the Hotel Excelsior.

HENDERSON: Who took the photograph?

MARIA: I did.

HENDERSON turns the photograph over and reads the writing on the back of the snapshot.

HENDERSON: Full marks, Miss Rocello.

HENDERSON takes a second photograph from the album.

MARIA: *(Surprised)* But where did you get the photograph from? And the album! It's my brother's!

HENDERSON:	(*Holding up the second photograph*) Who is this lady?
MARIA:	(*Surprised*) Why, she's my aunt of course.
HENDERSON:	And the photograph was taken where?
MARIA:	It was taken in Rome, outside her villa, about twelve months ago.
HENDERSON:	(*Pleasantly*) Thank you.

HENDERSON replaces the photographs in the album.

MARIA:	But what does this mean? (*Pointing to the album*) Where is the point of all this?
HENDERSON:	I'm sorry, but I had to make certain of something.
MARIA:	Certain – of what?
HENDERSON:	(*Looking at MARIA*) Of your identity, Miss Rocello.

HENDERSON crosses to the table and picks up the telephone.

OPERATOR:	(*On the other end of the line*) What number are you calling?
HENDERSON:	Will you get me Trunks, please?

MARIA crosses to HENDERSON.

MARIA:	(*Puzzled*) Mr Henderson, who are you? What was your connection with my brother?

HENDERSON looks at MARIA. He does not answer.

2nd OPERATOR:	(*On the other end of the line*) This is Trunks.
HENDERSON:	(*On the phone*) Will you get me a call to Liverpool, please? Central 1823. A personal call to Major Freece.
2nd OPERATOR:	Major Freexe?
HENDERSON:	That's right. Freece. F – R – E – E – C – E. My number is Medlow 18.
2nd OPERATOR:	Central 1823. Hold the line, please.
MARIA:	Mr Henderson, you haven't answered my question. Who are you? And who's this Major Freece you're telephoning?

HENDERSON: Major Freece is a friend of mine. Amongst other attributes he has a very persuasive tongue. (*Smiling*) I think he'll persuade you to return to Italy, Miss Rocello.

MARIA looks at HENDERSON. She is very puzzled.

CUT TO: INSPECTOR FORD's Office. Next morning.
FORD and DR SHELDON are sitting at the desk, discussing the medical report on BILLIE REYNOLDS. The foolscap report is in front of the INSPECTOR.

FORD: I don't see how you can be so certain that death was caused by strangulation, Doctor. There were definite marks on the throat, I admit, but the body has been in the water a week – maybe longer. Isn't it possible, therefore, –

SHELDON: (*Interrupting FORD, a shade irritable*) The marks were caused by someone taking Miss Reynolds by the throat and throttling her. I can give you a lot of high-faluting verbiage … but the plain fact of the matter is –

FORD: She was strangled.

SHELDON: Exactly!

FORD: Well, please don't think I'm trying to be difficult, but my superior, Superintendent Harringday, didn't think that your report was detailed enough.

SHELDON: (*Laughing*) Dr Jennings was right. The last thing he said to me was, "Remember, they won't be happy without a lot of fancy words, old boy."

FORD rises, smiles and holds out his hand.

FORD: All right, Doctor. Thank you for calling.

SHELDON: By the way, I don't know whether I ought to
                  tell you this, but Henderson came to see me.
FORD: (*Interested*) When?
SHELDON: Yesterday afternoon. He knew about the
                  Billie Reynolds murder and he wanted to
                  know how it happened.
FORD: How it happened?
SHELDON: Yes, he wanted to know the cause of death.
FORD: Did you tell him?
SHELDON: I told him she'd been murdered. That's all. I
                  said if he wanted further information, he'd
                  better talk to you.
FORD: (*Quietly*) Thank you, Doctor.

SERGEANT BRODERICK enters.

SHELDON: It seems to me he was pretty worked up about
                  something. It was almost as if … (*He
                  hesitates*)
FORD: Yes?
SHELDON: (*Shaking his head*) I mustn't let my
                  imagination run away with me. (*He picks up
                  his bag from the floor*) I've known Henderson
                  for quite a time now, and I like him. I think
                  Katherine likes him, too – which might make
                  it a little difficult, to say the least.
FORD: What do you mean?
SHELDON: Well, if you arrest Henderson for the Rocello
                  murder, Katherine's your principal witness,
                  isn't she?
FORD: (*A faint note of irritation in his voice*) We
                  haven't arrested him for anything – not yet.

SHELDON looks at FORD.

SHELDON: Er … no. Well, goodbye, Inspector. You
                  know where to find me.

BRODERICK opens the door and SHELDON nods to him and goes out.

BRODERICK: (*Closing the door*) Why was he talking about Henderson?

FORD: Henderson went to see him. Apparently he was curious about the medical report. (*Puzzled*) I don't understand this, Bob. If Henderson was responsible for the murder, or even mixed up in it, he must have known how Billie Reynolds died.

BRODERICK: He probably did know and was trying to pull the wool over our eyes.

FORD: Mmm-hm … Well, have you seen Miss Rocello?

BRODERICK: Yes, I've seen her, and I've got some news for you. She's flying back to Italy tomorrow morning.

FORD: (*Surprised*) Tomorrow morning?

BRODERICK: (*Nodding*) Yes, tomorrow morning.

FORD: But yesterday she was determined to stay here. Why when I even hinted that she should return she …

BRODERICK: (*Sitting down on the arm of the chair facing the desk*) Yesterday was yesterday. She's a different gal this morning.

FORD: What do you mean?

BRODERICK: You saw her last night. She was tense and worried. Today she's quite different. You wouldn't think it was the same girl.

FORD rises, comes round the desk and looks down at BRODERICK.

FORD: Why the change?

BRODERICK: I don't know.

FORD:	Didn't she give you an explanation? Didn't she say why she'd changed her mind?
BRODERICK:	She said she was quite happy to leave the whole affair in your hands. She said you impressed her … (*Imitating MARIA's accent*) very much.
FORD:	(*Puzzled; worried*) What the hell's this all about? This has happened since last night – since she saw Henderson.
BRODERICK:	(*Seriously*) Yes.
FORD:	(*A shade tense*) What happened last night?
BRODERICK:	I've told you, Mike.
FORD:	Tell me again.
BRODERICK:	Well, she went to see Henderson as arranged. She stayed at his flat about an hour. When she came out we picked her up and drove her down to the White Hart. She seemed a little excited, I thought, but rather reticent. Quite different from what she was this morning. I asked her how she got on, and she said that Henderson simply said that he was a friend of her brother's and if he could do anything to help her while she was in Medlow, he would.
FORD:	How did Henderson know that she was in Medlow in the first place?
BRODERICK:	Apparently young Craven told him – at least, that's what he told Miss Rocello.
FORD:	Mmm. Would you say she was sold on Henderson?
BRODERICK:	Oh, completely. I thought so last night. This morning I'm convinced of it.
FORD:	You think it's Henderson that's persuaded her to go back to Italy?
BRODERICK:	Yes, I do.

FORD: I'd like another word with the girl. Don't let
                   her leave Medlow without seeing me.
BRODERICK: (*Thoughtfully*) I'll phone her.
FORD: (*Smiling*) You look puzzled, Sergeant.
FORD sits on the corner of the desk.
BRODERICK: I am puzzled. (*Rising*) I know Henderson's
                   good looking, and educated, and got an
                   attractive personality and all the rest of it, but
                   I just don't see how he could put one over on
                   a girl like Maria Rocello. He must have told
                   her something last night, Mike. Something
                   which pleased her, and which really
                   convinced her that he was a friend of her
                   brother's.
FORD looks at BRODERICK.
FORD: (*Quietly*) Yes, but remember whatever he
                   said, it wasn't necessarily the truth.
*FORD crosses behind his desk as PC SANDERS enters carrying
an envelope.*
SANDERS: (*To FORD*) From Mr Stacey Boyd, sir.
FORD: (*Taking the envelope*) Thank you.
*SANDERS goes out. FORD opens the envelope and takes out a
sheet of notepaper. He reads the letter and frowns slightly.*
BRODERICK: What is it?
A moment, then FORD looks up.
FORD: You remember the note that Ralph Merson
                   received, with the earring?
BRODERICK: Yes, in Henderson's handwriting.
FORD: No, that's just it. (*He taps the letter he holds*)
                   Apparently it wasn't Henderson's
                   handwriting.
BRODERICK: But it was. It was the same handwriting on the
                   exercise book and on the note that young
                   Craven received.

147

FORD:	(*Shaking his head*) Not according to Mr Stacey Boyd, and he's the expert. He says the Craven note and the correction on the exercise book are the same handwriting. In other words they were written by Henderson, but he says the note to Ralph Merson is a copy – a good copy – but nevertheless a copy – of the same handwriting.
BRODERICK:	A copy of Henderson's handwriting.
FORD:	Apparently.
BRODERICK:	He must be mistaken.
FORD:	Well, if he's mistaken about this he could be mistaken about the others. (*He looks as the letter he is holding; quietly*) Somehow I don't think he is.

CUT TO: A Bedroom at the White Hart Hotel. Medlow.
MARIA ROCELLO is sat at a small writing bureau, writing a letter. She finishes the letter, blots it, and then places it in an envelope. As she is sealing the envelope there is a knock on the door and ROBIN CRAVEN enters. MARIA rises and turns away from the writing desk.

CRAVEN:	Miss Rocello?
MARIA:	(*Puzzled*) Yes.
CRAVEN:	I'm sorry to disturb you, Miss Rocello, but do you think you could spare me a few moments? I'm Robin Craven, the local correspondent of the London Despatch.
MARIA:	(*A shade annoyed*) What is it you want?
CRAVEN:	(*Pleasantly*) If you're busy I'll call back later. I don't wish to disturb you.
MARIA:	(*Relently*) No, if you've got any questions to ask you'd better ask them now.

CRAVEN enters the bedroom, closing the door behind him.

148

CRAVEN: You only arrived in Medlow yesterday afternoon, Miss Rocello, yet you're flying back to Italy tomorrow morning. Why?

MARIA: I'm sorry, I don't understand.

CRAVEN: Why such a quick visit? Have you already accomplished what you came for?

MARIA: How do you know I'm returning tomorrow morning?

CRAVEN: (*Smiling*) You've reserved a place on the 10.30 plane from London Airport.

MARIA: (*Quietly*) You appear to be well informed, Mr Craven.

CRAVEN: Not so well informed as I'd like to be. Miss Rocello, I wrote an article about your brother.

MARIA: Yes, I know, I read it.

CRAVEN: In that article I said your brother was a great friend of Count Paragi.

MARIA: Yes.

CRAVEN: Yesterday morning, for some obscure reason, The Times chose to contradict that statement. They said that your brother and Count Paragi were just wartime acquaintances. They quoted a recent statement, apparently made by Paragi, to that effect.

MARIA: Well?

CRAVEN: (*Smiling*) Well, I'd like to get the point clear. Am I right, or the illustrious Times? Was your brother a friend of Count Paragi's, or wasn't he?

MARIA: Either way I don't see that it's very important.

CRAVEN: Oh, but it is. The person who murdered your brother had a motive. In common with a lot of other people I'd like to know what that motive was.

MARIA: Would it help you if you knew whether my brother was a friend of Count Paragi's or not?

CRAVEN: (*Thoughtfully*) I think it might, Miss Rocello.

MARIA:	Well I'm sorry I can't answer your question.
CRAVEN:	(*Smiling, pleasantly*) You can't – or you won't?
MARIA:	I can't answer it because I don't know the answer. My brother had his own circle of friends. Whether Count Paragi was one of them or not, I don't know.
CRAVEN:	Did you ever meet Paragi?
MARIA:	Yes, once. About a year ago.
CRAVEN:	Where?
MARIA:	In Genoa.

The telephone rings.

CRAVEN:	Did your brother introduce you to him?
MARIA:	(*Hesitantly*) I can't remember who introduced me. (*Apparently dismissing CRAVEN*) Now, if you'll excuse me …

MARIA turns and picks up the telephone.

MARIA:	(*On the telephone*) Hello.
MAN:	(*On the other end of the telephone*) Miss Rocello?
MARIA:	Yes.
MAN:	Hold the line please, there's a call for you.

MARIA glances across at CRAVEN and is irritated to find that he is still present.

MARIA:	(*On the telephone*) Hello?
BRODERICK:	(*On the other end of the telephone*) Miss Rocello?
MARIA:	Yes.
BRODERICK:	This is Sergeant Broderick. Inspector Ford would like to see you before you leave. Do you think you could drop in sometime this evening?

While MARIA is on the telephone CRAVEN wanders round the room. He stops at the writing bureau and looks down at the envelope. After a moment he glances across at MARIA, then picks up the piece of blotting paper, folds it and puts it in his pocket.

MARIA: Well, I'm catching the 6.40 to London, and I don't want to –

BRODERICK: That's all right. Be here at 6 o'clock and I'll run you to the station.

MARIA: (*A moment's hesitation*) Yes, all right, Sergeant.

BRODERICK: (*Pleased*) Thank you, Miss Rocello.

CRAVEN returns to the centre of the room as MARIA finishes the phone call. MARIA replaces the telephone, turns, and sees CRAVEN who is now standing nearby.

CRAVEN: We were talking about Count Paragi. You were just going to tell me who introduced you to him.

MARIA: (*Faintly annoyed*) I don't remember who introduced me. It was at a cocktail party. I'm sorry, Mr Craven, there's nothing else I can tell you.

CRAVEN: (*Smiling, very pleasantly*) But you still haven't answered my question, Miss Rocello. Why are you returning home so soon?

MARIA: (*Hesitating*) I wanted to make sure that your police were making every effort to find my brother's murderer.

CRAVEN: And now you're satisfied?

MARIA: Yes. I've seen Inspector Ford and … I'm quite satisfied.

CRAVEN: What a pity you didn't telephone me. I could have saved you a journey.

MARIA: What do you mean?

151

CRAVEN: (*Smiling, yet with a faint note of sarcasm*) I
                could have told you – our police are
                wonderful – just wonderful!

CRAVEN smiles at MARIA.

CUT TO: The Drawing Room of DR SHELDON's House.
Afternoon.
*KATHERINE WALTERS is sitting on the settee, holding a
drawing board and adding the final touches to a dress design.
DR SHELDON enters carrying his medical bag. KATHERINE
puts the drawing board down on the settee and rises.*

SHELDON: Hello, Katherine.
KATHERINE: Mr Hobson's here. He's in the consulting
                room.
SHELDON: Yes, I know. Judy told me. (*Looks at the
                drawing*) What's that supposed to be?
KATHERINE: (*Smiling*) What does it looks like?
SHELDON: (*Just a shade puzzled*) Well it looks like a
                coat of some kind.
KATHERINE: (*Smiling*) It is a coat. That's the first drawing
                of mine you've recognised. One of us is
                improving.

SHELDON laughs.

SHELDON: Gosh, I could do with a cup of tea.
KATHERINE: I'll tell Judy.
SHELDON: No, I'd better see Hobson first. I've had quite
                a day, Katherine. I was with Ford nearly two
                hours. I shall be mighty glad when Jennings
                gets back.
KATHERINE: What did the Inspector have to say?
SHELDON: (*Puzzled*) He didn't say a great deal. I find
                Ford a very difficult man to weigh up.
KATHERINE: Does he still suspect Henderson?

SHELDON: (*Thoughtfully*) Yes, I think so, but he seems frightened to commit himself. Incidentally, I picked up a piece of gossip this morning. They say Rocello's sister's in Medlow, and that she saw Henderson last night.

KATHERINE: Who told you that?

SHELDON: (*A shade embarrassed*) Well actually I overheard the Inspector talking to Sergeant Broderick.

KATHERINE: (*Thoughtfully*) Rocello's sister?

SHELDON: Yes.

KATHERINE: I saw something in the paper this morning about a man called Harringday from Scotland Yard.

SHELDON: Yes. Ford's still in charge of the case, but he's answerable to Harringday. It was Harringday that complained about my report. The pompous ass didn't think it was detailed enough. (*A sigh*) Well, I suppose I'd better take a look at Mr Hobson. I expect he's coughing as well as ever.

KATHERINE: No, his cough's better.

SHELDON: (*Surprised*) It is.

KATHERINE: Yes.

SHELDON: Well, what's he called for?

KATHERINE: He's got sciatica.

SHELDON: Oh, my God!

KATHERINE laughs and picks up her drawing board. SHELDON goes into the consulting room. JUDY enters from the hall.

JUDY: (*To KATHERINE*) Mr Craven would like to see you, miss, if you can spare him a few minutes.

153

KATHERINE: (*Surprised*) Mr Craven? All right, Judy, ask him in.

JUDY leaves. KATHERINE puts her drawing board by the side of the settee, out of sight. ROBIN CRAVEN enters.

CRAVEN: (*Pleasantly*) Good afternoon.

KATHERINE: Hello, Mr Craven. Is it my uncle you want to see? Because if it is –

CRAVEN: No, no, I just wanted to ask your advice about something, Miss Walters.

KATHERINE: My advice?

CRAVEN: Well, I suppose you wouldn't call it advice really. It's just that I'd like you to do something for me. If you can, that is.

KATHERINE: What is it you want me to do?

CRAVEN: Do you speak Italian, Miss Walters?

KATHERINE: Yes, I do.

CRAVEN: (*Smiling*) Oh well, it shouldn't be difficult then.

KATHERINE is once again irritated by CRAVEN.

KATHERINE: What shouldn't be difficult, Mr Craven?

CRAVEN takes the piece of blotting paper out of his pocket.

CRAVEN: There's something written on this piece of blotting paper in Italian. I'd be awfully grateful if you'd translate it for me.

KATHERINE looks surprised, takes the blotting paper from CRAVEN and looks at it.

CRAVEN: (*Smiling*) You'll have to hold it up to a mirror, I'm afraid.

KATHERINE looks at CRAVEN, hesitates, then her curiosity gets the better of her, and she crosses to the mirror on the wall and holds up the piece of blotting paper. CRAVEN watches KATHERINE.

CRAVEN: Well? What does it say?

KATHERINE: It looks as if it's part of a letter.

CRAVEN takes a piece of paper and a pencil out of his pocket.

CRAVEN: Yes, it probably is. Can't you read it?

KATHERINE is staring at the letter in the mirror.

KATHERINE: (*Reading*) Yes, it says: "He's been very kind to me, and I consider it – er – (*Hesitantly*) a stroke of luck that I came here. I feel infinitely happier than I ever expected." … I think that's right. "I'll explain why when I" … It looks like – "when I see you."

KATHERINE turns from the mirror.

CRAVEN: (*The pencil on the paper*) Is that all?

KATHERINE: Yes. Yes, that's all. (*Puzzled*) Who wrote this? Why did you want me to translate it for you?

CRAVEN crosses and quickly takes the piece of blotting paper out of KATHERINE's hand.

CRAVEN: (*Glibly*) It was written by a friend of mine, and he lost the original. (*Smiling*) Still, it's most kind of you, Miss Walters. I'm very grateful. Give your uncle my regards.

CRAVEN quickly goes out. KATHERINE stands looking after him, puzzled and annoyed.

CUT TO: MARIA's Bedroom at the White Hart Hotel, Medlow.

MARIA is packing her suitcase, gathering various garments, etc. from the dressing table and the wardrobe. There is a knock on the door and MARIA looks up.

MARIA: (*Calling*) Come in.

There is a slight pause, and then the knock is repeated. MARIA puts down the dress she is holding, crosses and opens the door. KATHERINE WALTERS is standing in the doorway.

KATHERINE: (*Hesitantly*) Miss Rocello?

155

MARIA:	(*Puzzled*) Yes.
KATHERINE:	(*Pleasantly*) Could you spare me a few minutes? I'd very much like to have a word with you.
MARIA:	(*Cautiously*) Who are you? Are you a newspaper? Because if you are –
KATHERINE:	(*Laughing*) Do I look like a newspaper journalist? My name is Walters. Katherine Walters. I'm staying with my uncle Dr Sheldon. He has a practice in Medlow.
MARIA:	(*Still hesitant*) Well I have an appointment at six o'clock, I'm afraid.
KATHERINE:	What I've got to say won't take very long. I think it's in your interest that you should see me, Miss Rocello, as well as mine.
MARIA:	(*A moment, then*) All right, please come in.

KATHERINE enters the bedroom.

KATHERINE:	Miss Rocello, I'm going to ask you a rather strange question, but I've a very good reason for asking it. Did you write a letter this morning?
MARIA:	(*Surprised*) Why, yes.
KATHERINE:	Who was the letter to?
MARIA:	It was to my fiancé. He's in Paris and I wrote to say that – (*Suddenly, annoyed*) what business is it of yours whether I wrote a letter or not?
KATHERINE:	A man called Robin Craven came to see me this morning. He knew I spoke Italian, so he asked me to translate something for him.
MARIA:	(*Puzzled*) Well?

KATHERINE looks towards the desk.

KATHERINE: (*Slowly*) The words he asked me to translate were on a piece of blotting paper. I have a feeling it was taken from your desk.

MARIA stares at KATHERINE, then quickly turns and crosses to the writing bureau. She sees part of the blotting paper is missing. She turns back towards KATHERINE.

MARIA: (*A note of tenseness in her voice*) What was on the blotting paper?

KATHERINE: (*Pleasantly*) Don't worry, Mr Craven wasn't as lucky as he might have been. It simply said, "He's been terribly kind to me, and I consider it a stroke of luck that I came here. I feel much happier than I did. I'll explain why when I see you."

MARIA: (*Faintly relieved*) Is that all it said?

KATHERINE: (*Nodding*) Yes, that's all.

MARIA: (*Quietly*) Thank you for telling me, Miss Walters.

KATHERINE: Miss Rocello, please don't think I'm being impertinent but who were you referring to when you said "He's been terribly kind to me."

MARIA: I was referring to someone I've met since I've been down here.

KATHERINE: Was it David Henderson?

MARIA: (*Surprised*) What do you know about David Henderson?

KATHERINE: I know that at any moment he's likely to be arrested and I shall be a witness.

MARIA: (*Puzzled*) What do you mean?

KATHERINE: I saw Henderson the afternoon your brother was murdered. I saw him leave the houseboat.

MARIA: (*Surprised*) David Henderson?

KATHERINE: Yes.

MARIA:	You must be mistaken.
KATHERINE:	(*Seriously; worried*) No, I'm not mistaken.

MARIA looks at KATHERINE. There is the faint suggestion of a smile on her face.

MARIA:	I met Henderson last night for the first time. He seemed a very nice man. (*Slowly; still the suggestion of a smile*) Somehow, I don't think he murdered my brother.
KATHERINE:	Was it Henderson you were referring to in your letter?
MARIA:	(*Nodding*) Yes, it was Henderson. (*Before KATHERINE speaks*) But please, now I would like to ask you a question, Miss Walters, if you don't mind.
KATHERINE:	Yes, of course.
MARIA:	It's a rather personal question. I hope you don't think I'm being impertinent.
KATHERINE:	No. no, of course not.
MARIA:	Are you in love with him?
KATHERINE:	(*Amazed*) In love with him? With David Henderson?
MARIA:	Yes.
KATHERINE:	(*With an embarrassed little laugh*) Good gracious, no! Why, I've only seen the man twice.
MARIA:	(*Slowly, looking at KATHERINE*) What has that got to do with it?

KATHERINE meets MARIA's gaze, then very slightly turns away from her. MARIA still has the faint suggestion of a smile on her face.

CUT TO: INSPECTOR FORD's Office.

FORD is sitting behind his desk, writing a report. There is a cup of tea on the desk by the writing pad. The INSPECTOR pauses for a moment as if lost for a word, glances at his watch, and then continues writing. BRODERICK enters and as he does so the telephone starts to ring.

BRODERICK: Miss Rocello's here.

FORD: All right, I'll see her in a minute.

FORD picks up the telephone receiver.

FORD: (*On the telephone*) Hello.

CUT TO: HARRY VINCENT in a telephone box.

VINCENT is a pleasant, capable looking man of about fifty.

VINCENT: (*A pleasant voice, pulling FORD's leg*) Is that Detective Inspector Ford?

FORD: Speaking.

VINCENT: *The* Detective Inspector Ford?

CUT TO: INSPECTOR FORD's Office.

FORD: (*Irritated*) Yes, what is it?

CUT TO: The Telephone Box.

VINCENT: (*Laughing*) You haven't lost your bark, Inspector. Still the same old charmer.

FORD: (*A shade angry*) Who the devil is that?

VINCENT: (*Still amused*) Don't you recognise the dulcet tones of Harry Vincent?

CUT TO: INSPECTOR FORD's Office.

FORD: (*Astonished and delighted*) Good Lord, Harry Vin … Hello, Harry! Where are you? Where the devil are you speaking from?

VINCENT: I'm in a call box at Henley, on my way up North. I thought we might have dinner together, for old times' sake.

FORD: I'd love to, Harry.

159

CUT TO:	The Telephone Box.
VINCENT:	I'll pick you up at the office in about half an hour.

CUT TO:	INSPECTOR FORD's Office.
FORD:	Fine. Oh … how's the ticker?

CUT TO:	The Telephone Box.
VINCENT:	(*A thought, then*) Oh, much the same. Still misses a beat when it feels like it. See you in about half an hour.

CUT TO: INSPECTOR FORD's Office.

FORD, smiling to himself, replaces the telephone receiver. He looks up and sees BRODERICK watching him.

FORD:	That was Harry Vincent. Did you ever meet him?
BRODERICK:	No, but I've often heard you speak of him.
FORD:	He's a wonderful character. We used to be great friends in the old days.
BRODERICK:	He retired, didn't he? About eighteen months ago.
FORD:	Yes, it was a damn shame. He was just coming up for promotion. He'd have been a Chief Inspector by now, then his heart went dicky on him.
BRODERICK:	What's he been doing?
FORD:	I don't know. Someone told me he had a part time job with a commercial firm. (*Rising*) All right, Bob, I'll see Miss Rocello now.

BRODERICK opens the door and speaks to MARIA who is in the adjoining room.

BRODERICK:	Would you come in please?

MARIA enters.

160

FORD: (*Looking at MARIA, stern but not unfriendly*) Sergeant Broderick tells me that you're returning to Italy almost immediately.

MARIA: (*Smiling*) Yes, Inspector. I'm taking your advice.

FORD: (*Indicating the chair opposite his desk*) You didn't seem very keen on taking my advice yesterday afternoon. You said you intended to stay here until the case was solved – until we found the person who murdered your brother.

MARIA sits in the chair. FORD returns to his position behind the desk.

MARIA: Yes, I know I said that yesterday, Inspector, but I've changed my mind.

FORD: Why?

MARIA: (*With a little shrug*) I've thought the matter over, and I've come to the conclusion there's nothing I can do. There's just no reason for my staying here.

FORD: (*Leaning forward*) Miss Rocello, this decision of yours has been taken since you saw David Henderson.

MARIA: Yes, I know, but not as a – what is the word – not as a result of my interview with Mr Henderson.

FORD: I find that difficult to believe.

MARIA: (*Smiling*) You don't have to believe it, Inspector.

FORD: (*A shade angry*) What did Henderson say to you last night? What did he tell you?

MARIA: I've already told the Sergeant about my interview with Mr Henderson.

FORD: You've told the Sergeant precisely nothing!

MARIA: Mr Henderson said he was a friend of my brother's and that he was convinced you were doing everything in your power to solve the case. He was very nice about you, Inspector.

FORD:	That's interesting. Very interesting. You see, Henderson told me, and Sergeant Broderick, that he didn't know your brother, that he'd never even seen him.
MARIA:	(*A moment, hesitating*) Well, I'm sorry, that's not what he told me.
BRODERICK:	Go on, Miss Rocello. What else did he tell you?
MARIA:	Er – nothing else.
FORD:	But you were with Henderson almost an hour. You must have talked about something!
MARIA:	(*Lightly*) We talked about – Florence, Rome, Venice – and about boats, Inspector.
FORD:	(*Surprised*) Boats?
MARIA:	(*Smiling*) Yes, boats.
FORD:	(*Faintly exasperated*) What kind of boats?
MARIA:	(*Lightly*) Just boats, Inspector. Sailing boats.
FORD:	But why on earth talk about sailing boats?
MARIA:	Why not? We're both very fond of sailing boats.

FORD looks at BRODERICK, as much as to say, "I give this up."

FORD:	(*Grimly determined*) Now look, Miss Rocello, I don't want to be difficult, but –
MARIA:	(*Interrupting FORD, with a pleasant smile*) I don't want to be difficult, either, Inspector, but I would like to catch the six-forty train, if possible.

FORD looks at MARIA, obviously exasperated then suddenly changes his mind and rises.

FORD:	I think it's a very good idea.

MARIA rises. BRODERICK takes her by the arm and leads her towards the door. FORD sinks back into his chair.

MARIA:	Goodbye, Inspector, and thank you.

FORD: Thank you, Miss Rocello.

Maria goes out and the door closes. FORD looks puzzled, bewildered and a little exasperated. He strokes his chin, then turns, stirs his cup of tea and lifts up the cup.

CUT TO: DAVID HENDERSON's Study at Buckingham College. Early evening.

HENDERSON is sat at the desk, consulting the BILLIE REYNOLDS diary. He makes an occasional note on a piece of notepaper. There is a knock on the door and MRS WILLIAMS enters. HENDERSON turns.

MRS WILLIAMS: Excuse me, sir, there's a Mr Merson to see you.

HENDERSON: Oh yes, Mrs Williams. Ask him in, please.

MRS WILLIAMS goes out and HENDERSON rises and crosses down towards the door. RALPH MERSON enters. He is obviously puzzled and a little suspicious.

HENDERSON: Mr Merson?

MERSON: Yes.

HENDERSON: I'm David Henderson. It's very good of you to call. Do sit down, sir.

MERSON remains standing. He takes a note out of his coat pocket.

MERSON: Look, Mr Henderson, I don't know who you are, or what this is all about, but I would like –

HENDERSON: (*Interrupting MERSON*) I'm a Housemaster at Buckingham College – that's the large building on the right, just as you enter the gate.

MERSON: (*Impatiently*) I know Buckingham College. Now what's the meaning of this note?

HENDERSON: It means I'd like to talk to you. I thought that was obvious.

163

MERSON: What is it you want to talk to me about?

HENDERSON: About Miss Reynolds. Miss Billie Reynolds.

MERSON looks distinctly worried.

MERSON: I – I don't know anyone called Reynolds.

HENDERSON: Don't you? Then you have a very short
               memory. (*Smiling*) On Thursday, July 5th you
               took Miss Reynolds to the first house at the
               London Palladium. On Friday, August 3rd you
               went down to Brighton and met Miss
               Reynolds at the Grand Central Hotel. You
               stayed there, with Miss Reynolds, until
               Tuesday, August 7th.

MERSON: (*With sarcasm*) You seem to be very well
               informed.

HENDERSON: I make a point of it.

MERSON: (*Very angry*) Well suppose you make a point
               of getting to the point. What the hell's this all
               about?

*HENDERSON looks at MERSON then suddenly his manner
changes. He speaks with obvious authority.*

HENDERSON: I want something from you, Mr Merson. And
               I want it now. Tonight.

MERSON: (*Nervously*) What is it you want?

HENDERSON: (*After a tiny pause*) Information.

MERSON: (*Surprised*) Information?

HENDERSON: (*Nodding*) Yes. What did Miss Reynolds call
               you? Did she use your Christian name or had
               she a nickname for you?

MERSON: Look here, what business is it of yours what
               Billie Reynolds called me?

HENDERSON: I'm asking you a question, Mr Merson, and
               strange though it may seem, it's a very
               important one. (*With authority*) What did
               Miss Reynolds call you?

164

MERSON:	(*Hesitantly*) Well if you must know, she called me Toffee. (*Aggressively*) And if you want to know why she called me Toffee …
HENDERSON:	(*Calmly, shaking his head, unconcerned*) I don't. You've answered my question, and I'm satisfied.

MERSON looks at HENDERSON with a new interest. He sits on the arm of the settee.

MERSON:	(*Quietly*) You knew the answer, didn't you?
HENDERSON:	I knew that Miss Reynolds was friendly with someone she called Toffee, but I wasn't sure who it was.
MERSON:	Well, it was me. Now have you any other questions you'd like to ask?
HENDERSON:	Yes, I have.

HENDERSON crosses and picks up the diary from the desk.

HENDERSON:	You see this diary?
MERSON:	Yes.
HENDERSON:	It belongs to Billie Reynolds.
MERSON:	(*Rising, shocked*) Good God!
HENDERSON:	(*Smiling*) There's a lot of interesting information in this diary, Mr Merson, including several references to a gentlemen called R.
MERSON:	(*Interested*) R?
HENDERSON:	Yes.
MERSON:	You mean the initial R?
HENDERSON:	(*Nodding, quietly*) Yes. (*He opens the diary, looks at MERSON and then slowly reads from the diary*) "R. came to see me soon after it was dark. I wish I didn't feel this way about him. I just don't know whether to trust him or not." (*He looks up*) Who was she referring to? Do you know?

165

MERSON:	(*A shade tense*) No. No, I don't.
HENDERSON:	Did she ever mention anyone to you whose name – presumably Christian name – began with the letter R?
MERSON:	(*Thoughtfully, puzzled*) No, I can't think of anyone.
HENDERSON:	(*Watching MERSON*) You're sure?
MERSON:	(*A shade angry*) Yes, I'm quite sure. (*Tense*) Where did you get that diary from?
HENDERSON:	I got it from a gentleman called Chris Reynolds. He was a little reluctant to part with it, but he did.
MERSON:	And what are you going to do with it?
HENDERSON:	I'm going to keep it. For the time being.
MERSON:	(*Tensely, worried*) Look, Henderson, let's be perfectly frank with each other. I'm mentioned in that diary. I must be. So, obviously –
HENDERSON:	You are. You are indeed.
MERSON:	(*Grimly*) Well, I'll give you two thousand pounds for it.
HENDERSON:	(*Politely*) Two thousand pounds. (*He looks at the diary, smiles at MERSON*) I should have thought it was worth much more than that, Mr Merson.

HENDERSON looks at the diary he is holding in his hands.

CUT TO: INSPECTOR FORD's Office. Evening.
FORD is standing by the desk, tidying up for the night, placing documents in drawers, cupboards, etc. The door opens and HARRY VINCENT pops his head into the room.

VINCENT:	May I come in?
FORD:	(*Delighted*) Hello, Harry! Yes, of course! Come in, old man!

VINCENT enters, closing the door behind him. The two men shake hands.

VINCENT: Well, Mike, it's been a long time …

FORD: It certainly has! I'm delighted to see you, you old war horse! (*Surprised*) By George, you look well, Harry. You don't look as if you've got a care in the world.

VINCENT: (*Laughing*) I wouldn't say that. How's Roger?

FORD: Oh, he's fine. Sit down, old man. Roger's at Buckingham College, you know. He took a scholarship.

VINCENT sits. FORD returns behind the desk and takes out a box of cigars.

VINCENT: Yes, I heard about that.

FORD: Well, what have you been doing with yourself? What's it like to be a retired flatfoot?

VINCENT smiles and takes a cigar. FORD offers him a light.

VINCENT: You seem to be in the news these days, Mike.

FORD: (*Thoughtfully*) Yes, we've quite a case on our hands. But let's not talk shop. What about you? What have you been doing with yourself?

VINCENT: (*Smiling*) I've been abroad for six months.

FORD: Have you? On holiday?

VINCENT: Ostensibly.

FORD: How's the heart? Does it still trouble you?

VINCENT looks at his cigar.

There is a slight pause.

VINCENT: It never did trouble me, Mike. It's always been pretty good.

FORD: But I thought that was why you retired – because you'd got a weak heart?

VINCENT: Yes, I know. A lot of people thought that.

FORD looks puzzled. VINCENT looks at his cigar again.

VINCENT: Mike, I came up from London specially to see you.

FORD: To see me?

VINCENT: Yes, I'm on my way up North.

FORD: Oh. Oh, I see.

VINCENT: I wonder if you do see, Mike?

FORD: (*Curious*) Is something the matter, Harry?

VINCENT: No, there's nothing the matter, except that I'm afraid you're in for one or two surprises.

FORD: Surprises? Me?

VINCENT: Yes. (*Smiling*) To start with, I never did have a weak heart, and I didn't retire.

FORD: But you did. Dammit, we had a dinner! I made a speech. We gave you a silver salver.

VINCENT: Yes, I know. I've always felt a little guilty about that salver.

FORD rises. He is obviously bewildered.

FORD: Look, Harry – are you serious?

VINCENT: Perfectly serious.

FORD: Well, if you <u>didn't</u> retire what the hell did you do?

VINCENT: I was put in charge of a new Department.

FORD: A new Department? At Scotland Yard?

VINCENT: Well, not exactly at Scotland Yard, Mike. I'm working with Sir Edward Westerby.

FORD: Sir Edward Westerby!

VINCENT nods.

FORD: But he's the Head of M.I.5.

VINCENT: Yes, I know.

FORD stares at VINCENT.

FORD: (*Quietly*) Good God, Harry, are you in the Secret Service?

VINCENT looks at HARRY, then starts to laugh.

VINCENT: You know, it's a curious thing, whenever I hear those two words I always think of the Bing Boys – William Le Queux – Zeppelins – and Charlie

Chaplin in Shoulder Arms. (*Still amused*) Did you
ever see Shoulder Arms?

FORD: You haven't answered my question.

VINCENT: I don't propose to answer it, either. (*Pleasantly*) I
didn't come here to answer questions, Mike.

FORD: (*Quietly*) What did you come for?

VINCENT: (*A moment, looking at FORD*) I came to tell you
something.

FORD: What?

*VINCENT rises and stands by the desk, looking down at the
blotter.*

VINCENT: (*Quite simply*) Rocello isn't dead, you know.

FORD: (*Astonished*) Isn't dead?

VINCENT: No.

FORD: You mean Paul Rocello – the Italian? The man that
was murdered?

VINCENT: (*Smiling*) Yes, except that he wasn't murdered.

FORD: But, good God, man, I saw the body!

VINCENT: You saw a body, but not Rocello's.

FORD: (*Bewildered*) Harry, are you sure? Do you know
what you're saying?

VINCENT: I'm saying that Rocello isn't dead. As a matter of
fact, he's in Canada. (*Looks at his watch*) Or he will
be within the next four or five hours.

FORD sits in the chair facing the desk, obviously bewildered.

VINCENT: Mike, I'd like you to meet someone. He's waiting in
the outer office.

FORD: (*Looking up*) Yes, of course. But who is it?

VINCENT crosses to the door.

VINCENT: He's a colleague of mine. (*Smiling*) We call him –
The Other Man.

FORD: The Other Man?

*VINCENT opens the door and beckons to someone outside.
FORD rises and turns towards the door.*

169

VINCENT: You can come in now.
FORD looks towards the open door.

END OF EPISODE FIVE

EPISODE SIX

OPEN TO: INSPECTOR FORD's Office. Evening.

DETECTIVE INSPECTOR FORD is sitting at his desk facing HARRY VINCENT. Ford looks bewildered and puzzled.

VINCENT: Mike, I'd like you to meet someone. He's waiting in the outer office.

FORD: Yes, of course. But who is it?

VINCENT crosses to the door.

VINCENT: He's a colleague of mine. (*Smiling*) We call him – The Other Man.

FORD: The Other Man?

VINCENT opens the door and beckons to someone outside. FORD rises and turns towards the door.

VINCENT: You can come in now.

DAVID HENDERSON enters; he is carrying a hat and a pair of gloves and looks completely at ease.

FORD: Henderson!

HENDERSON crosses and shakes hands with the INSPECTOR.

HENDERSON: Hello, Inspector!

VINCENT closes the door. FORD looks at HENDERSON then across at VINCENT.

HENDERSON: (*To VINCENT*) Well – have you told him?

VINCENT: I've told him about Rocello – that's all.

HENDERSON: Well, if you don't mind, Mr Vincent, I'd like you to tell him the rest of the story.

FORD: Look, before we go any further. I know you didn't murder Rocello because he isn't dead, but ...

HENDERSON: I didn't murder anyone, Inspector, although there's a certain gentleman I'd gladly murder if I could get my hands on him.

FORD looks at HENDERSON.

FORD: (*To VINCENT*) Harry, don't you think you'd better tell me the rest of this story?

173

VINCENT sits in the chair facing the desk. FORD indicates the other chair for HENDERSON.

VINCENT: (*Smiling at HENDERSON*) Yes, I've a shrewd suspicion that if I don't, Henderson will.

VINCENT takes out his cigarette case and offers FORD and HENDERSON a cigarette; they refuse so VINCENT puts a cigarette in his mouth and replaces the case. He leans forward to accept a light from FORD.

VINCENT: Thank you, Mike. Well, I suppose the best place to start any story is at the beginning. (*To FORD*) Does the name Kirbydale mean anything to do?

FORD: No.

VINCENT: It was the name of a naval tanker. On the 10th of September 1941 it was lying at anchor in Gibraltar. Suddenly, to everyone's astonishment, it was blown sky high. After investigation we knew Count Paragi and Paul Rocello were responsible.

FORD: (*Interested*) Go on, Harry.

VINCENT: Paragi and Rocello were pioneers in underwater warfare, they invented the limpet bomb and had a great deal to do with the launching of the first human torpedo. When the war was over Rocello continued to be interested in naval warfare, he also became very friendly with Henderson who, unknown to Rocello, was attached to M.I.5.

FORD: Go on …

VINCENT: I was working for Naval Intelligence at the time and Henderson sent me a report. He said that Rocello had started work on a new project, an apparatus to combat Briggs D. Now Briggs D. was an explosive which was used for underwater vibration work.

FORD: (*Stopping VINCENT*) Now wait a minute,
                 Harry! Don't get technical – I don't even
                 know how my fridge works.

HENDERSON laughs.

HENDERSON: Let me put it in simple language, Inspector.
                 During the war when a ship detected enemy
                 Frogmen or human torpedoes they used depth
                 charges; but a very special kind of depth
                 charge. It was called Briggs D.

FORD: I see.

HENDERSON: It produced a series of underwater
                 convulsions, vibrations if you like, and
                 everything – literally everything set within a
                 certain radius was killed instantaneously.

FORD: I'm beginning to get this. Rocello was
                 working on apparatus which would defeat
                 Briggs D, which a Frogman could wear, in
                 fact, as a sort of – well – antidote.

HENDERSON: (*Smiling*) Exactly.

VINCENT: Well, this work of Rocello's went on for
                 some years. About six months ago however
                 one of our agents – a man called Cooper …

FORD: (*Nodding*) I know Cooper …

VINCENT: … Reported that certain other people were
                 interested in Rocello's experiments. It was
                 then that we decided to bring Henderson into
                 the picture.

HENDERSON: (*To FORD*) I went to Italy and persuaded
                 Rocello to continue his experiments in this
                 country.

VINCENT: But Rocello wasn't completely safe, not even
                 here, so we decided that the only thing to do
                 was to give the impression he was dead – that
                 he had in fact been murdered. A body was

	planted and Henderson sent an anonymous note to a local journalist – Robin Craven.
HENDERSON:	We knew that Craven would put two and two together, get excited about the Frogman story and give us all the publicity we needed.
FORD:	I see. Then the night that Billie Reynolds saw you …
HENDERSON:	We were planting the dead man. Rocello had already left for Liverpool.
FORD:	But that was in the early hours of the morning. The following afternoon Katherine Walters saw you …
HENDERSON:	Yes.

HENDERSON looks at VINCENT.

VINCENT:	Cooper, who was in charge of the operation, forgot Rocello's wristlet watch. It was flown down from Liverpool and Henderson went back to the houseboat with it.
FORD:	I see. (*Looking at HENDERSON*) And Billie Reynolds?
VINCENT:	Well, Billie saw too much and we had a nasty feeling that she might guess what was going on. Also she was friendly with a man we suspected – a man we'd had our eye on for some little time.
FORD:	(*Surprised and interested*) A local man?
VINCENT:	Yes. We took Billie away from Medlow and put her in a flat in Chelsea. Naturally, we couldn't explain the true position – we had to make up a story. Unfortunately, she didn't do as she was told and she gave us the slip. Although we can't prove it we're pretty sure she wrote to this friend of hers and eventually saw him.

176

FORD: The one you mentioned?

VINCENT: Yes.

FORD looks at VINCENT then across to HENDERSON.

FORD: Who is this man, do you know?

HENDERSON takes Billie Reynolds' diary out of his pocket and hands it to the INSPECTOR.

HENDERSON: Well, Billie refers to him in her diary simply as 'R'.

FORD: (*Taking the diary and looking at it, puzzled*) 'R'?

HENDERSON: Yes.

FORD: (*Quietly, to VINCENT, looking up from the diary*) Is he an agent?

VINCENT: (*Nodding*) Yes, he's an agent all right, he was watching Rocello.

FORD: And you say he was a local man?

VINCENT: Yes.

FORD: Well – have you any idea who he is?

VINCENT: Yes, we've a pretty good idea – but it's catching the gentleman.

FORD rises; obviously perturbed.

FORD: Good God, Harry, we've got to catch him – he's a murderer!

VINCENT: (*Nodding*) That's why we're here. We've all got to pull together on this, Mike.

CUT TO: INSPECTOR FORD's Office. The next morning.

FORD is sitting at his desk writing a note: the telephone rings and he stops writing and lifts the receiver.

MAN: (*On the other end of the telephone*) I've got Dr Sheldon on the line, sir.

FORD: (*On the telephone*) Thank you.

SHELDON: (*On the other end of the telephone*) Hello – this is Dr Sheldon speaking …

177

FORD:	Good morning, doctor. Inspector Ford here.
SHELDON:	Oh, yes, Inspector – what can I do for you?
FORD:	I've had another memo through about the Reynolds report, sir. Do you think you could drop in and see me sometime this afternoon?
SHELDON:	Yes, I think so. Four o'clock?
FORD:	That'll do nicely. I'll look forward to seeing you then.

FORD replaces the receiver, presses a button on his desk, then completes his note. He puts the note in an envelope, sticks it down and addresses it. PC SANDERS enters.

FORD:	(*Handing SANDERS the note*) See this is delivered to a Mr Vincent. The address is on the envelope.
SANDERS:	Yes, sir.
FORD:	Is Sergeant Broderick …

BRODERICK enters.

FORD:	Oh, hello, Bob! (*To SANDERS*) There's no need to wait for a reply.
SANDERS:	Very good, sir.

SANDERS goes out, leaving the door slightly ajar.

FORD:	(*To BRODERICK*) Sit down.
BRODERICK:	Morgan said you wanted to see me.
FORD:	Yes, I do.

FORD rises, moves behind BRODERICK and carefully closes the door.

BRODERICK:	(*Curious*) Has something happened?
FORD:	(*Turning from the door*) Yes. I've got something to tell you – about the Rocello case.

FORD returns to his seat at the desk.

BRODERICK:	Oh – what is it?

FORD looks at BRODERICK for a moment, hesitating.

FORD:	Don't waste any more time on Henderson.

BRODERICK: (*Puzzled*) What do you mean?

FORD is busy locking certain drawers in his desk.

FORD: I mean Henderson's out – he's no longer a suspect.

BRODERICK: (*Bewildered*) No longer a … Good God, Mike, he's our principal suspect! If we cross Henderson off our list, where are we?

FORD: (*Looking up from the desk, a touch of authority*) Bob, listen – you've got to accept what I'm telling you without question. Henderson's out.

BRODERICK: You mean – completely?

FORD: Yes.

BRODERICK: You mean – he'd nothing to do with Rocello or the Reynolds murder?

FORD: That's right.

BRODERICK: (*Still bewildered and puzzled*) But I can hardly believe that. (*A thought*) Have you seen Henderson?

FORD: Yes.

BRODERICK: When?

FORD: Last night.

BRODERICK: And he convinced you that he'd nothing whatever to do with …

FORD: (*Interrupting BRODERICK; a shade curt*) He convinced me completely.

BRODERICK: Well, what did he say? What did he tell you?

FORD: (*Looking down at some papers on his desk*) He produced an alibi.

BRODERICK: (*Incredulously*) But, Mike, if Henderson's had an alibi all this time why hadn't he …

FORD: (*Interrupting BRODERICK; rising and moving round the desk*) Bob, I've told you. Henderson's out. He's off the list. No more.

179

BRODERICK looks at FORD, still puzzled: he obviously doesn't believe the alibi story.

BRODERICK: All right, you're the boss – but don't expect me to believe that story.

FORD: What do you mean?

BRODERICK: If Henderson's had an alibi why hasn't he produced it before now? (*Shaking his head*) I don't pretend to understand this, Mike – maybe it's none of my business, but …

FORD: But what?

BRODERICK: (*Looking at FORD*) You don't believe all this nonsense about an alibi either, I'm sure of that. Something's happened – something pretty big.

FORD hesitates, smiles and gives BRODERICK a little pat on the shoulder.

FORD: Let's leave it like that.

BRODERICK: (*Accepting the decision*) Well – if Henderson's off the list, where do we go from here?

FORD returns to his desk; opens a drawer and takes out the Reynolds diary.

FORD: Billie Reynolds kept a diary – in this diary she made several references to a man she called 'R'. (*He holds up the diary*) 'R's' the man we're after – he's the man who killed her.

BRODERICK: Are you sure of this?

FORD: I'm positive.

BRODERICK: (*Thoughtfully*) R … (*He suddenly looks up*)

FORD: You're thinking of Merson – Ralph Merson?

BRODERICK: Yes.

FORD: (*Shaking his head*) She had a nick name for Merson.

BRODERICK: How do you know?
FORD: (*Pointing to the diary*) It's in the diary.
BRODERICK: (*Quietly*) May I see that, Mike?
FORD: Yes, of course.
FORD hands BRODERICK the diary.
BRODERICK: Thanks.
BRODERICK sits holding the diary; slowly going through the pages. FORD watches him for a little while.
FORD: What are you looking for?
BRODERICK: I'm looking to see if she was ill at any time
                 …
FORD: Ill?
BRODERICK: (*Still looking at the diary*) Yes, I wondered
                 who her doctor was.
FORD: You're thinking of Sheldon?
BRODERICK: Yes, I don't know why. It was just a thought.
FORD: (*Thought*) Dr Richard Sheldon …
BRODERICK continues to examine the diary.

CUT TO: DAVID HENDERSON's Study at Buckingham College. Morning.
HARRY VINCENT is sitting in an armchair watching HENDERSON who is standing by the window. VINCENT is pressing tobacco into his pipe.
HENDERSON: (*Turning*) I still think it would be very much
                 safer if you used one of your own people.
VINCENT: (*Taking out his lighter*) I don't agree. If
                 Craven's caught there's an outside chance
                 they'll consider he's just a snooper – the local
                 newshound trying to dig up something for his
                 paper.
HENDERSON: Contrary to general belief journalists don't
                 usually break into other people's houses.

VINCENT: I know that. But supposing I did use one of my men and 'R' recognised him?

HENDERSON: Yes, that would be a difficult situation, I admit.

VINCENT: 'R' would be out of the country before we could say knife. This way we've nothing to lose, providing Craven keeps his head.

HENDERSON: How did he react to the suggestion?

VINCENT: (*Smiling*) He was a little taken aback, but he'll do it all right. I asked him to call round and have another talk about it.

HENDERSON: (*Nodding*) Did you get the handkerchief you wanted?

VINCENT: They're sending one down from Town.

HENDERSON: What have you promised Craven – exclusive rights in the Rocello story?

VINCENT: (*Lighting his pipe; looking up at HENDERSON*) When the time comes he'll get the story all right.

The doorbell rings. HENDERSON looks at VINCENT then crosses to the door and opens it. A UNIFORMED MESSENGER stands in the doorway.

MESSENGER: Mr Vincent?

VINCENT crosses to the door.

VINCENT: Yes?

MESSENGER: A message from Inspector Ford, sir.

The MESSENGER hands VINCENT the note written by FORD.

VINCENT: Oh, thank you.

The MESSENGER salutes and turns away. HENDERSON closes the door. VINCENT opens the note.

VINCENT: (*After reading the note; looking up*) Ford's seeing Sheldon at four o'clock.

HENDERSON: (*Nodding*) In that case I'd better make certain she's going to be in.

VINCENT: Yes.

HENDERSON crosses and picks up the telephone.

OPERATOR: (*On the other end of the telephone*) Number,
                please?
HENDERSON: (*On the telephone*) Medlow 158 …
OPERATOR: One moment, sir …

*There is a pause, then we hear the number ringing out. After a
little while the receiver is lifted.*

CUT TO: DR SHELDON's House.

KATHERINE: (*On the telephone*) Medlow 158 …
HENDERSON: (*On the other end of the telephone*) Miss
                Walters?
KATHERINE: Yes.

CUT TO: DAVID HENDERSON's Study.

HENDERSON: This is David Henderson. How are you, Miss
                Walters?

CUT TO: DR SHELDON's House.

KATHERINE: (*A little surprised*) I'm – very well, thank you.

CUT TO: DAVID HENDERSON's Study.

HENDERSON: Miss Walters, I'd rather like to have a little
                chat with you – will you be in this afternoon?
KATHERINE: Yes, I think so.
HENDERSON: Well, I'll drop in for a cup of tea about four
                o'clock.

CUT TO: DR SHELDON's House.

KATHERINE: (*Taken aback*) Er – yes, yes, all right, Mr
                Henderson.
HENDERSON: Goodbye.
KATHERINE: Goodbye.

CUT TO: DAVID HENDERSON's Study.

HENDERSON: (*Smiling to himself; just before she rings off*) Oh, and Miss Walters …

KATHERINE: Yes?

HENDERSON: Nothing elaborate, just a few sandwiches, scones, the odd cake or two. (*He puts down the receiver*)

CUT TO: DR SHELDON's House.

KATHERINE looks at the receiver in her hand, dumbfounded, then suddenly she starts to smile.

CUT TO: DAVID HENDERSON's Study.

HENDERSON, having just replaced the receiver, turns towards VINCENT who is burning FORD's note with his cigarette lighter.

VINCENT: (*Dropping the ashes into the wastepaper basket*) What are you going to tell that girl?

HENDERSON: (*A shade surprised*) Why – what we've arranged to tell her – what you suggested.

VINCENT: Yes, but – anything else?

HENDERSON: What do you mean?

VINCENT: Wouldn't you like to tell her the whole story, so far as you're concerned?

HENDERSON: Obviously, but I can't, not without your permission.

VINCENT: (*Looking at HENDERSON; quietly*) Well – my permission rather depends.

HENDERSON: On what?

VINCENT: Is this the last time, Henderson – the last time you're prepared to work for us?

HENDERSON: Yes, I've already told you that. I wouldn't have helped you this time only – well, I was

	curious about Rocello and the Briggs D. experiments.
VINCENT:	Yes. (*He strolls across to the window; stands looking out at the view*) Are you happy down here, then?
HENDERSON:	Extremely happy. I want to stay that way.
VINCENT:	(*Turning*) You didn't feel like that ten years ago. You said you'd do anything – anywhere – at any time.
HENDERSON:	Who told you that?
VINCENT:	Sir Edward Westerby; I saw the letter you wrote him.
HENDERSON:	(*Shaking his head*) I didn't write that letter. The other man wrote it – the man I told you about – the square peg in the round role.
VINCENT:	(*Moving across to HENDERSON*) Sir Edward asked me to find out if you'd be interested in joining my department. I'd like to have you, Henderson.
HENDERSON:	You don't want me, you want the other man – and he's dead. I buried him the day I came to Medlow. (*Smiling*) Besides, I'm too soft for your department, Vincent. I'm the amateur tucked away in his little backwater.

The doorbell rings.

VINCENT:	I've heard that before. All right, Henderson. Tell your girlfriend the whole story – but keep me out of it.
HENDERSON:	She's not my girlfriend!
VINCENT:	(*Smiling; indicating the door*) That's probably Craven.

HENDERSON looks at VINCENT, hesitates, then crosses to the door. VINCENT watches him; sucking his pipe.

185

CUT TO: The Drawing Room of DR SHELDON's House.
Afternoon.

*KATHERINE WALTERS is sitting on the settee, she is obviously
deeply interested in what DAVID HENDERSON is saying.*

HENDERSON: … If Cooper hadn't forgotten the wristlet
             watch there wouldn't have been any necessity
             for me to go back to the houseboat – and you
             wouldn't have seen me.

KATHERINE rises from the settee.

KATHERINE: But why didn't you tell me this at the time?
             I'd never have gone to the police.

HENDERSON: (*Smiling*) I couldn't, Miss Walters, I was
             sworn to secrecy. In any case, if I'd told you
             about the watch you'd have guessed that the
             dead man wasn't Rocello.

KATHERINE: Where is Rocello now?

HENDERSON: He's in Canada.

KATHERINE: And is his work – what you were telling me
             about – is it completed then?

HENDERSON: So far as we're concerned, yes. You see, the
             first part of his work, the most important
             experiments – could only take place in
             Europe, that's why we had to be sure that he
             wasn't going to be interfered with – why we
             wanted certain people to think he'd been
             murdered.

KATHERINE: I see. (*Thoughtfully*) Mr Henderson, you
             remember the evening you came to see my
             uncle about your shoulder?

HENDERSON: Yes.

KATHERINE: It was me you really wanted to see, wasn't it?

HENDERSON: Yes. We knew there was an agent in the
             district watching Rocello and we thought
             perhaps …

186

KATHERINE: (*Surprised*) You suspected me?

HENDERSON: We weren't sure. You'd just come back from the Continent – you were on the river – perhaps watching the houseboat.

KATHERINE: (*Thoughtfully*) Yes, of course.

HENDERSON: But we don't suspect you any longer, Miss Walters. Otherwise I wouldn't have invited myself to tea.

KATHERINE smiles, looks at HENDERSON, then hesitates.

HENDERSON: What were you going to say?

KATHERINE: I was going to say – do you mind if I ask a very personal question?

HENDERSON: No, please.

KATHERINE: Are you a schoolmaster?

HENDERSON: Why, yes, of course.

KATHERINE: Or – are you really with M.I.5.?

HENDERSON: (*Smiling*) If I was with M.I.5. I wouldn't be talking to you like this.

KATHERINE: You might – if you had an ulterior motive.

HENDERSON: (*Shaking his head*) I'm a Housemaster at Buckingham College; I've every intention of remaining one.

KATHERINE: Then how on earth did you get mixed up in all this?

HENDERSON: During the latter part of the war I was attached to Naval Intelligence. That's when I first met Rocello. When this business blew up they asked me to take a hand in it because, well – because I was a friend of Rocello's and I knew a little bit about what he was trying to do.

KATHERINE: I see.

HENDERSON: It's my first and last assignment, Miss Walters – if that's what you're thinking.

187

KATHERINE: It's really no concern of mine, I was just curious.

HENDERSON: (*Smiling*) I understand you saw Maria Rocello while she was in Medlow?

KATHERINE: Yes, a man called Robin Craven called me to translate a message that she'd written …

HENDERSON: Yes, I know.

KATHERINE: Did Craven tell you?

HENDERSON: No, Maria telephoned me just before she left.

KATHERINE is remembering her interview with MARIA.

KATHERINE: Oh.

HENDERSON: (*Watching HENDERSON*) She said you'd been to see her – she was very grateful.

KATHERINE: Oh, it was nothing. It was the obvious thing for me to do. (*Suddenly; changing the subject*) Well, now this is all over you'll be returning to your …

HENDERSON: (*Seriously*) I'm afraid it isn't all over – not yet.

KATHERINE: What do you mean?

HENDERSON looks at KATHERINE for a moment; he moves to a small table and thoughtfully picks up one of the ashtrays.

HENDERSON: I said just now there was an agent in Medlow – a man watching Rocello.

KATHERINE: Yes?

HENDERSON: He's still here.

KATHERINE: How do you know?

HENDERSON: Because we know who it is.

KATHERINE: (*Surprised*) You know …?

HENDERSON: (*Quietly; looking at the ashtray*) Yes, Miss Walters.

KATHERINE: (*A sudden realisation*) Is this the man that murdered Billie Reynolds?

HENDERSON: (*Looking up at KATHERINE; nodding*) Yes.
                (*He puts the ashtray down on the table*) I
                want to talk to you about him; that's why I
                came here.

*HENDERSON crosses to KATHERINE and as he does so there is
a knock and the door opens. KATHERINE turns towards the
door. JUDY enters wheeling a tea trolley which is laden with
pastries, scones, sandwiches, bread and butter, muffins, etc.
HENDERSON stares at the trolley in amazement. KATHERINE
watches him, amused by his expression. He looks up, catches her
eyes, and gives a self-conscious little smile.*

CUT TO: DAVID HENDERSON's Study. Afternoon.
The curtains are drawn and the lights are on.
*VINCENT is standing near the window, looking out between a
gap in the curtain. His manner is tense and he is obviously a
shade worried. HENDERSON is sitting in an armchair watching
him, there is a magazine on his lap and an ashtray with a pile of
cigarette ends on the arm of the chair. VINCENT turns and looks
at his watch.*

VINCENT: Something happened. It's a quarter to three.
                Craven should have been here an hour ago.
HENDERSON: Supposing we drive round to the house?
VINCENT: We'll give him another fifteen minutes, if
                he's not here by then we'll do that.
HENDERSON: Right. (*Rises*) Would you like a drink?
VINCENT: Yes, I think I would.

*HENDERSON crosses to the drinks table and mixes VINCENT a
whisky and soda. VINCENT looks at his watch again.
HENDERSON brings the drink to VINCENT.*

VINCENT: Thanks. (*Still studying his watch*) He left here
                just after twelve … (*Looking up*) How long
                would it take him to get here?
HENDERSON: About twenty minutes.

189

VINCENT:	Well, say he was at the house at half past … Half an hour to get the lay of the land, then fifteen minutes for …
HENDERSON:	(*Quickly; tensely*) Wait a minute!
VINCENT:	What is it?
HENDERSON:	There's a car coming!

They stand listening. Gradually the sound of an approaching car can be heard and the lights from the headlamps flicker across the window. HENDERSON crosses to the window and looks out.

| HENDERSON: | (*Turning*) It's Craven! |
| VINCENT: | Good! |

HENDERSON crosses to the door and opens it, then returns to VINCENT. They stand watching the door.

After a little while ROBIN CRAVEN enters. He wears a black mackintosh, dark trilby, gloves, rubber plimsolls and carries a small manuscript case. There is a blood stained handkerchief wrapped round his left hand. He looks tense and a shade exhausted.

HENDERSON:	(*Friendly*) What happened, Craven? You're terribly late.
CRAVEN:	My God, I should think so! What a night!
VINCENT:	You've cut your hand.
CRAVEN:	It's nothing, it's just a scratch but it wouldn't stop bleeding.
VINCENT:	Well – what happened?
CRAVEN:	Breaking into the house was easy – I had no difficulty at all. Everything went like clockwork, just as we planned it.
VINCENT:	Well?
CRAVEN:	I was in one of the bedrooms having a jolly good look round when – damn me if he didn't walk straight in!
HENDERSON:	What happened?

CRAVEN: (*Smiling*) Fortunately I'd heard him coming, by the time he'd opened the door and switched the light on I was behind the wardrobe. I had to stay behind that blasted wardrobe best part of an hour!

HENDERSON smiles. CRAVEN crosses to VINCENT and hands him the document case. VINCENT immediately opens it.

HENDERSON: You're sure he didn't see you?

CRAVEN: Yes, I'm quite sure.

HENDERSON: And what about the handkerchief?

CRAVEN: (*Nodding*) That's all right – that was the first thing I did.

HENDERSON and CRAVEN turn and look at VINCENT who is now studying several letters and a photograph, taken from the document case.

CRAVEN: They were in a cupboard in the bedroom. I had to force it open.

VINCENT nods; obviously very pleased.

VINCENT: Good work, Craven.

HENDERSON: (*To VINCENT; cautiously*) Is it what you wanted?

VINCENT gives HENDERSON a significant nod.

HENDERSON: (*To CRAVEN*) I expect you feel like a drink?

CRAVEN: I certainly do.

HENDERSON: What would you like – a whisky and soda?

CRAVEN: Thank you.

VINCENT: (*Looking up from a letter he is reading*) Give him a double – he's earned it.

CRAVEN looks distinctly pleased with himself.

CUT TO: DETECTIVE INSPECTOR FORD's Office. Morning.

FORD is sitting at his desk writing a letter, occasionally he pauses and glances at his watch. After a little while voices can be heard in the outer office; angry voices. FORD looks up listening; finally he rises and crosses to the door.

MERSON: (*From the outer office*) I'm not interested in your instructions! I demand to see the Inspector!

SANDERS: (*Also in the outer office*) I'm sorry, sir. The Inspector can't be disturbed at the moment.

MERSON: (*Off*) What do you mean – he can't be disturbed? Of course he can! Who the hell does he think he is – the Prime Minister?!

FORD opens the door.

FORD: (*Pleasantly*) Come along in, Mr Merson.

RALPH MERSON enters looking distinctly annoyed and irritated. He glances back at SANDERS who is hovering in the doorway.

SANDERS: I'm sorry, sir.

FORD: That's all right, Sanders.

FORD closes the door.

MERSON: I've been waiting in that confounded office since nine o'clock.

FORD: Yes, I know. I've had rather a busy morning. (*Indicating a chair*) What can I do for you, Mr Merson?

MERSON looks at FORD, hesitates, then:

MERSON: (*Bluntly*) Did you break into my house last night?

FORD: (*Quietly*) Me?

MERSON: (*Irritably*) I don't necessarily mean you, personally.

FORD: Well, what do you mean?

MERSON: I mean, one of your men – one of your staff.

FORD: (*Casually; picking up a ruler*) Why should we break into your house, Mr Merson?

MERSON: I don't know why! I'm asking you if you did.

FORD: Haven't you got hold of the wrong end of the
                stick? We're supposed to prevent people from
                breaking into houses.

MERSON: (*Angrily*) Somebody broke into my house last
                night – they searched the place from top to
                bottom.

FORD: Did they take anything?

MERSON: (*Hesitantly*) It's difficult to tell, I don't think so.

FORD: (*Looking at MERSON over the ruler*) Then you
                were very fortunate.

MERSON: Look, Ford, I'm going to be very frank with you.

FORD: You're doing pretty well as it is.

MERSON: (*Leaning across the desk*) I've a hunch you think
                I murdered Billie Reynolds. I think you searched
                my house last night – looking for something.

FORD: Looking for what?

MERSON: Well – (*He hesitates*)

FORD: Go on, Mr Merson.

MERSON: Well, it's my guess you were looking for the
                weapon.

FORD: What weapon?

MERSON: The weapon that killed Billie Reynolds.

FORD: But she was strangled, you know that – it's been
                in all the newspapers.

MERSON: Yes, I know, but they say she was strangled with
                something, a rope – a piece of cord perhaps.

FORD: And you think that's what we were looking for?

MERSON: Well – it's a possibility.

FORD: When did you discover that your house had been
                broken into?

MERSON: This morning, about seven o'clock – I saw the
                broken glass near the French windows.

FORD: Why didn't you phone us straightaway?

MERSON: Because nothing seemed to be missing and I …
            didn't want my wife to hear.

FORD puts down the ruler and rises from the desk.

FORD: Well, I didn't break into your house, Mr Merson,
            and I didn't instruct anyone else to do so.

MERSON: (*Obviously relieved*) Oh …

FORD: If you ask me you've been reading too many
            detective novels, and not very good ones either.

SERGEANT BRODERICK enters.

FORD: (*To BRODERICK*) Someone broke into
            Merson's house last night. Take Morgan and see
            if there are any fingerprints. The usual routine.

BRODERICK: (*To MERSON*) When did this happen?

MERSON: I don't know, it must have been sometime during
            the night.

FORD: (*To BRODERICK*) Let me know how you get on.

BRODERICK: Yes, sir.

*BRODERICK and MERSON go out. FORD returns to his desk;
after a moment the door opens again and BRODERICK returns.*

BRODERICK: I didn't want to say anything in front of Merson;
            we've had a report on Chris Reynolds.

FORD: Well?

BRODERICK: Apparently he's back in Town: he's working for
            a greengrocer on the Edgware Road.

FORD: Find out how he spent the last twenty-four hours.
            Get in touch with the Yard if necessary.

BRODERICK: Right.

*BRODERICK goes out. FORD turns, picks up a cigarette and
then his lighter. Suddenly he changes his mind and throws the
cigarette down on the desk. He looks thoughtful; rather worried.*

CUT TO: DETECTIVE INSPECTOR FORD's Office.
Early evening of the same day.

SANDERS is standing by the desk taking documents out of the 'Out' tray and placing letters, papers, etc, in the 'In' tray. SERGEANT BRODERICK enters; he is wearing a coat and carrying his hat.

BRODERICK: (*To SANDERS*) Where's the Inspector?

SANDERS: I don't know. He went out just after four. I haven't seen him since.

BRODERICK: Do you know whether he's coming back this evening?

SANDERS: No, but I should imagine he is. His son phoned about five minutes ago.

BRODERICK: Roger?

SANDERS: Yes. He's not feeling too good – got pains in his stomach or something. My God, these kids are all the same!

FORD enters; he is wearing his coat and hat and his manner is brisk and a shade terse.

FORD: What's this, a committee meeting?

BRODERICK: No, I just wanted to …

FORD crosses to his desk and takes a document from the 'In' tray.

FORD: (*Interrupting BRODERICK; to SANDERS*) Has Superintendent Harringday phoned?

SANDERS: No, sir.

BRODERICK: Roger's been on the phone, he's not well.

FORD: (*Immediately looking up*) When was this?

SANDERS: About five minutes ago, sir. He said he'd got pains in his stomach and was going to bed.

FORD: (*Dismissing SANDERS*) Yes, all right, Sanders.

SANDERS goes out. FORD throws the document down on the desk.

FORD: That's just what I needed! I've had a hell of a day!

BRODERICK:	You look as if you could use a drink.
FORD:	(*Looking at his watch*) I'm supposed to be seeing Miss Walters at six o'clock.
BRODERICK:	I'll see her if you like; if it's important I'll give you a ring.
FORD:	Yes, all right, Bob. I'll be at home.
BRODERICK:	What does she want, do you know?
FORD:	I haven't the slightest idea, she simply rang and said she wanted to see me.
BRODERICK:	I'll sort it out. I hope the boy's all right, Mike.
FORD:	It's an extraordinary thing, this always happens when he's on holiday. During term he's as right as nip.
BRODERICK:	(*Smiling*) Too many ices and too much television.
FORD:	I wouldn't be surprised. Oh, by the way, how did you get on at Merson's?

BRODERICK sits on the corner of the desk; he is obviously perplexed.

BRODERICK:	Well, to be honest I can't quite figure it out. There's a pane of glass out of the French windows and it certainly looks as if someone broke in, but – (*Dubiously*) I don't know.
FORD:	Fingerprints?
BRODERICK:	(*Shaking his head*) Nothing. Nothing at all.
FORD:	Did anyone hear anything?
BRODERICK:	There's only Merson and his wife, they didn't hear a thing.
FORD:	What about Chris Reynolds – did you check?
BRODERICK:	Yes, he's in London. He hasn't been down here for days.
FORD:	M'm. (*Turning towards the door, then suddenly hesitating*) Oh – did you see Mrs Merson?

BRODERICK:	Yes, I saw her.
FORD:	(*Curious*) What's she like?
BRODERICK:	(*At a complete loss for words*) Well – (*Thoughtfully, pulling the lobe of his right ear*) – quite different from Billie Reynolds.
FORD:	(*Laughing*) Yes, I thought she might be. Give me a ring if you want me.

FORD goes out.

CUT TO: The Drawing room of DR SHELDON's House. Night.

The curtains are drawn and the lights are on.

The doorbell rings. The consulting room door opens and KATHERINE enters. JUDY enters from the hall with SERGEANT BRODERICK. JUDY is wearing a hat and coat and carries a handbag.

JUDY:	Sergeant Broderick to see you, miss.
KATHERINE:	Oh, come in, Sergeant.
BRODERICK:	Good evening, Miss Walters.
KATHERINE:	Are you off now, Judy?
JUDY:	Yes, miss.
KATHERINE:	Now make sure you've got your key this time.
JUDY:	(*Grinning*) Yes, Miss Walters.

JUDY smiles at BRODERICK and goes out.

BRODERICK:	(*To KATHERINE*) Inspector Ford asked me to call round, Miss. He said you telephoned him this afternoon.
KATHERINE:	Yes, that's right, I did.

A slight pause.

KATHERINE:	Isn't the Inspector coming then?
BRODERICK:	No, I'm afraid he couldn't make it. (*Smiling*) That's why I'm here.
KATHERINE:	Oh ...

BRODERICK: His son's been taken ill.

KATHERINE: Oh, I'm sorry to hear that.

BRODERICK: I don't think it's serious. (*Pleasantly*) Well, what can we do for you, Miss Walters?

KATHERINE: (*Frowning*) I really think I ought to speak to the Inspector about this, Sergeant – it's rather important.

BRODERICK: (*Indicating the telephone*) Well, I can send for him if you think it's necessary, Miss.

KATHERINE: Well …

BRODERICK: Can't you give me some idea what it's all about?

KATHERINE gives a little glance towards the door leading into the hall.

KATHERINE: It's about my uncle.

BRODERICK: (*Quietly, surprised*) Your uncle – Dr Sheldon?

KATHERINE: Yes.

BRODERICK: What about Dr Sheldon?

KATHERINE: I've found out something about him – something that the Inspector – well, the police – ought to know about.

BRODERICK: Go on, Miss Walters.

There is the sound of the front door opening and closing.

KATHERINE: Two days before Billie Reynolds disappeared … my uncle … (*She stops; turns towards the door*)

BRODERICK looks towards the hall. DR SHELDON enters; he is wearing his hat and overcoat and carries his medical bag as well as the small document wallet carried by CRAVEN in an earlier scene. He appears very harassed and has apparently been running.

KATHERINE: (*Quickly*) What is it? What's happened?

SHELDON immediately crosses to the telephone.

198

BRODERICK: What's the matter, doctor?

SHELDON: (*Picking up the telephone receiver*) There's been a car accident at Medlow Bridge, both drivers are very badly hurt … (*To KATHERINE*) Katherine, there's a hypodermic on my desk, fetch it …

KATHERINE rushes into the consulting room.

SHELDON: (*Tapping the receiver*) What's the matter with this confounded thing?

BRODERICK: What happened exactly?

SHELDON: God knows, I've never seen a crash like it. A car hit one of those gravel lorries from Henley quarry. (*Impatiently; tapping the receiver*) What the hell is the matter with this?

BRODERICK: Who was in the car, do you know?

SHELDON: A chap called Berson – or Merson – or something like that, anyway he's in a pretty bad way.

BRODERICK: Merson? Ralph Merson?

KATHERINE hurries out of the consulting room with the hypodermic box in her hand.

KATHERINE: Is this it?

SHELDON: Yes, that's it, Katherine. (*He quickly hands BRODERICK the telephone; crosses, takes the box from KATHERINE, and puts it in his bag. To BRODERICK*) Get St Peter's Hospital. Medlow 22 – Extension 4. Tell them what's happened and tell them it's urgent.

BRODERICK nods and starts tapping the receiver.

BRODERICK: (*On the telephone*) Operator!

SHELDON hands KATHERINE the document case.

SHELDON: This must have been thrown out of the car. It belongs to the driver. Take care of it until I get back.

SHELDON goes out.

BRODERICK: (*On the telephone*) Operator! (*Turning to KATHERINE*) There's something the matter with this thing!

KATHERINE: It was perfectly all right this afternoon.

BRODERICK: It sounds dead to me. (*He continues tapping the receiver*) Operator!

KATHERINE is opening the document case; she takes out a photograph and several envelopes; she takes a letter out of one of the envelopes and looks at it.

BRODERICK: (*Turning towards KATHERINE*) I think I'd better go down to a phone box, this thing … is … obviously … (*He stops, watches KATHERINE for a moment and then slowly replaces the receiver*)

KATHERINE looks up.

BRODERICK: Where did you get that letter from?

KATHERINE: It was in this case. It's addressed to you – it's from Billie Reynolds. (*She looks at the letter: Reads*) "Dear Robert, I'm staying in London but I must see you …"

BRODERICK: Give me that – give me that letter!

BRODERICK moves towards KATHERINE who instinctively moves away from him. BRODERICK stops. KATHERINE stops, she is still facing him.

KATHERINE: There's also a photograph of you – with Billie Reynolds.

BRODERICK: Yes, I know – those things were taken from my house last night. They belong to me. (*Holding out his hand*) Now give them to me, Miss Walters, please.

KATHERINE moves again putting a chair between herself and BRODERICK.

KATHERINE: Why should Miss Reynolds want to meet you – was she a friend of yours?

BRODERICK: Miss Walters, it's none of your business – now give me the letters and the photograph.

KATHERINE: (*Looking at the other envelopes*) You appear to have quite a few friends on the Continent, Mr Broderick. Germany – Czechoslovakia – Hungary …

BRODERICK suddenly kicks over the chair.

BRODERICK: Give me those letters!

KATHERINE has moved away again behind the central table.

KATHERINE: (*Shaking her head*) These are for Inspector Ford – no one else.

BRODERICK: (*Quietly, yet intensely angry*) Give me those letters …

BRODERICK moves towards KATHERINE and she moves again, watching him, trying to foretell his movements.

BRODERICK: (*Softly*) Miss Walters, I'm warning you, if you don't do what I tell you I'll …

KATHERINE: (*Her eyes glued on BRODERICK*) You'll what, Mr Broderick? (*She moves round the table*)

BRODERICK watches KATHERINE as he moves slowly round the table.

KATHERINE: You killed Billie Reynolds, didn't you?

BRODERICK: I want those letters …

KATHERINE: (*Tensely*) You killed Billie Reynolds, didn't you?

BRODERICK is now standing by the standard lamp.

BRODERICK: (*Suddenly, losing his temper*) Yes, I did. I killed the little bitch. She started asking questions – all sorts of questions … (*He*

reaches out and rips the sashcord off the
standard light)

KATHERINE moves back slightly towards the door.
BRODERICK advances towards her, slowly twisting the
sashcord round his fingers.

BRODERICK: Now, Miss Walters, don't be stupid about
this. No one's seen those letters or the
photograph, except you and Merson. If you'll
give them back to me …

KATHERINE suddenly turns the central table over, completely
taking BRODERICK by surprise; she then rushes across to the
light switch near the door.

The moment the room is plunged into darkness KATHERINE
races across to the window and vanishes behind the curtain.

BRODERICK trips over the table, curses, then rushes to the light
switch.

BRODERICK switches the lights back on again. He is tense and
angry as he looks round the room for KATHERINE. He sees the
movement of the curtain and realises where she has gone.
Gripping the sashcord between his fingers he slowly advances
towards the French windows.

Suddenly BRODERICK springs forward, grabs the curtain and
tears it down. He finds himself face to face with HENDERSON.

BRODERICK: (*Staggered*) Henderson! What are you doing
here?

BRODERICK falls back into the room; HENDERSON following
him.

HENDERSON: Since you appear to be under a
misapprehension, Sergeant – I thought I'd
explain a few things to you.

202

BRODERICK:	What do you mean?
HENDERSON:	Well, to start with. Those letters you want – and the photograph.
BRODERICK:	Well?
HENDERSON:	Quite a few people have seen them by now, but not – curiously enough – Mr Merson.
BRODERICK:	Don't be a damn fool, Merson took them from my room last night!
HENDERSON:	(*Shaking his head*) No, you thought he did – that's why you broke into his house. But it wasn't Merson.
BRODERICK:	(*Angrily*) I tell you it was! I found a handkerchief with his initials on it, I … (*He stops, stares at HENDERSON, retreats further back into the room*) My God, was this a trap? The whole thing? The whole story about Merson …?

BRODERICK quickly turns towards the consulting room, then stops dead. FORD has come out of the consulting room and is watching him.

BRODERICK stands in the centre of the room, looking first at FORD then at HENDERSON. Suddenly he smiles, takes something out of his pocket and puts it in his mouth. HENDERSON springs forward in an attempt to get his arm, but he is too late. The SERGEANT sinks down onto the arm of the settee and puts his hand over his eyes.

HENDERSON:	(*To FORD*) He's taken something, get Sheldon – quickly!

FORD moves across to the French windows and immediately he does so BRODERICK springs to life and throws HENDERSON to one side, and dashes into the consulting room, slamming the door behind him.

HENDERSON:	Damn!

HENDERSON and FORD rush to the consulting room door but BRODERICK has already locked it. HENDERSON proceeds to throw his weight against the door and FORD turns and rushes out through the French windows. From inside the consulting room comes the sound of the window being smashed.

Suddenly excited voices and the sound of a struggle are heard in the garden and after a moment FORD walks back into the room through the French windows.

FORD: (*To HENDERSON*) It's all right – we've got him.

The consulting room door is unlocked and opened by a plainclothes man; he nods to FORD and then remains in the room.

HENDERSON moves to the settee. As FORD turns to go Dr SHELDON enters through the French windows with KATHERINE. He is holding her arm.

FORD: (*Pleasantly, to SHELDON*) Thank you, doctor – you've been most cooperative. (*He smiles at KATHERINE*) And you too, Miss Walters.

KATHERINE: Don't ever ask me to do anything like that again!

FORD: We won't, Miss – don't worry. (*To SHELDON*) I think you'd better take a look at your consulting room, sir. He's made rather a mess of the window.

SHELDON: Yes, I think I'd better.

SHELDON crosses to the consulting room.

SHELDON: (*To HENDERSON*) Get Katherine a drink, Henderson, and help yourself. (*To FORD*) I expect you could do with one, Inspector?

FORD: No, thank you sir. I must be off.

SHELDON goes into the consulting room.

FORD: (*To HENDERSON*) Can I give you a lift?

HENDERSON: Er – no, Inspector, I think I'll walk.

FORD looks at HENDERSON, then at KATHERINE, gives a little smile to himself and goes out. HENDERSON crosses to the drinks cabinet.

HENDERSON: What would you like?

KATHERINE: (*Hesitantly*) I don't think I'll have anything.

HENDERSON: (*Turning*) Really?

KATHERINE: Yes, really.

HENDERSON turns and joins KATHERINE.

HENDERSON: I expect you're still feeling pretty shaky.

KATHERINE: (*With a little smile*) I'm all right.

HENDERSON: Were you frightened?

KATHERINE: (*Nodding*) Terrified.

HENDERSON: So was I.

KATHERINE laughs.

There is a slight pause, HENDERSON appears thoughtful.

KATHERINE: (*Watching HENDERSON; seriously*) What are you thinking of – Broderick?

HENDERSON: No, curiously enough I was thinking of a family motto.

KATHERINE: Motto?

HENDERSON: Yes. Rocello's. (*He looks at KATHERINE*) Survitor in modo, fortiter in re …

KATHERINE: (*Thoughtfully; translating*) Gentle in the manner …?

As she speaks HENDERSON nods and pulls KATHERINE gently towards him.

HENDERSON: But vigorous in the deed!

HENDERSON suddenly takes KATHERINE in his arms and kisses her. They hold the embrace.

THE END

Francis Durbridge and *The Other Man* by Harold Santon

On Saturday there begins on television a new Francis Durbridge serial, and that name in the billing of a programme has by now become a guarantee and a hallmark – serials from this master of the noble and ancient art of "cliffhanging" are as distinctive as Hitchcock films or Turkish cigarettes. Through the imperishable Paul Temple, who began a hectic life on radio as far back as 1938, Francis Durbridge became a familiar name, made even more familiar over the last five years by equally exciting television serials – *The Broken Horseshoe, Operation Diplomat, The Teckman Biography, Portrait of Alison* and *My Friend Charles.*

The Other Man is a little different from his previous serials. The scene has moved out of London and the West End to a fictitious small town called Medlow. Like Mr Durbridge's previous home town, Walton-on-Thames, it is situated by a river – most essential to the plot.

This time the central character, David Henderson, house master of a public school, is not trying to clear his name. On the contrary, he seems to be incriminating himself by doing very suspicious things – we see him doing them. Why? That is the question, and one doesn't have to be a seer to prophesy that we shall be kept in agonising suspense for the answer until the last few minutes of the last episode.

Though the name of Durbridge and the flavour of his writing have become so familiar, the man himself has remained rather indistinct in the background. He is forty-three years old, youthful looking in spite of a rapidly balding head, rather short and broad.

Just when Mr Durbridge decided to become a writer is uncertain, but it must have been at a very early age. He had his first play, a mystery-thriller called *The Great Dutton*, put on for charity when he was only fifteen years old and still a pupil at school outside Birmingham.

At Birmingham University he wrote and played in a revue before an audience which included Martyn C. Webster. Mr Webster was not impressed with Francis Durbridge as an actor, but he was pleased to produce a serious play, called *Promotion*, which Durbridge wrote soon after leaving University. It went out from the BBC Midland studios and was so successful that it was presented three times and the sequel *Dolmans* was commissioned.

The idea of a new detective character called Paul Temple was developing in Durbridge's mind and there came the day in 1938 when he took the script of the first serial, *Send For Paul Temple*, to Martyn C. Webster.

It went out in the Midlands with a repeat over the London wavelengths, and by the end of the last episode Durbridge had broken all records for drama fan mail. Paul Temple went on from strength to strength, moved from the radio to the novel and from Britain to overseas. Will he get on to television? "I haven't decided yet," says Mr Durbridge. But there is another BBC television serial to be written for some time next year, so it's always possible.

Printed in Great Britain
by Amazon